BELMONT CASTLE

BELMONT CASTLE

or

SUFFERING SENSIBILITY

Theobald Wolfe Tone
&
divers hands

Edited by

MARION DEANE

THE LILLIPUT PRESS
DUBLIN

Edition copyright © The Lilliput Press, 1998
Introduction and notes copyright © Marion Deane, 1998

First published 1998 by
THE LILLIPUT PRESS LTD
62-63 Sitric Road, Arbour Hill,
Dublin 7, Ireland.

A CIP record for this
title is available from
The British Library.

ISBN 1 901866 06 8

The Lilliput Press receives financial assistance from
An Chomhairle Ealaíon/The Arts Council of Ireland.

Set by Sheila Stephenson in New Baskerville with notes in Futura Light
Printed in Ireland by ßetaprint of Clonshaugh, Dublin

CONTENTS

ATTRIBUTION OF AUTHORSHIP

Theobald Wolfe Tone
Letters III, VI, VIII, IX, XII, XIV, XVI, XVII, XIX, XXIII, XXV,
XXVI, XXVII, XXVIII, XXIX, XXX, XXXII, XXXIV

John Radcliffe
Letters I, II, IV, V, X, XXI, XXII, XXXI, XXXIII, XXXV

Richard Jebb
Letters VII, XI, XIII, XV, XVIII, XX, XXIV

INTRODUCTION

One may wonder why *Belmont Castle* has lain in relative obscurity for over two hundred years. There are several reasons for this. In the first place, the only known surviving copies were in private hands until the 1930s. Since the National Library of Ireland copy was catalogued in 1935, a number of scholars, bibliographers and journalists have alluded to the book's existence.[1] They were presumably looking for evidence that would throw additional light on the personality and career of Theobald Wolfe Tone, the most famous of its three co-authors. But they seemed to find in the novel little more than a further example of that 'execrable trash' which Tone claimed to satirize.[2] From the point of view of the literary scholar, *Belmont Castle* is of interest as a minor example of the sentimental novel of the late eighteenth century; but it seems to offer little more than that. I, however, would like to show that it is a much more interesting text than a purely literary or bibliographical perspective would suggest.

In brief, this is a *roman-à-clef*. Internal evidence, combined with evidence from the lives of the three authors, reveals that *Belmont Castle* is a veiled account of real events in their personal affairs and in the enclosed world of several famous and interconnected families of the Anglo-Irish ruling class. The possibility of a libel action against the authors or their publisher was raised in the one known review of the novel, printed in *The Universal Magazine and Review or Repository of Literature* in November 1790:

... we cannot avoid expressing our disapprobation of the almost uncharitable severity with which the Editor has treated several of the most distinguished characters both in this and in the sister kingdom ... True it is, the portraits of these personages have a strong resemblance to their originals, but as caricatures they should be discountenanced.[3]

On 7 August 1796 Tone recorded in his diary:

[1]

I … In conjunction with two of my friends, named Jebb and Radcliffe, wrote a burlesque novel, which we called *Belmont Castle*, and was intended to ridicule the execrable trash of the Circulating Libraries.[4]

Close examination of the text confirms Tone as the central contributor.
Radcliffe creates background, while Jebb fills in sketches of characters
supplied by Tone and Radcliffe; the figure of Sir James Dashton is his only
unique contribution.[5] The trio regarded the novel as an elaborate joke,
accessible only to that privileged section of society which could afford to
laugh at the foibles of celebrated colleagues or of those who aspired to
friendship with them. To make the joke effective, it was necessary to establish a code of gentlemanly propriety that would place indiscreet or outrageous behaviour in high relief. It was Radcliffe who, in the note from
the 'Editor', undertook to establish this.

Jebb, Radcliffe and Tone were all graduates of Trinity College, Dublin,
who found themselves in London to read for the Bar at the Inns of
Temple in 1787. It was at this time that the joint venture of writing an epistolary novel was first mooted. Each of them had, by background and education, an interest in literature, the plastic arts, theatre, music, and specif-
ically the newly fashionable Italian opera. Their original aim seems to
have been to parody the popular sentimental fiction of the period, but
they eventually combined this with the idea of caricaturing well-known
members of their social group.

Jebb and Radcliffe completed their legal studies and later held prominent positions in the Anglo-Irish establishment. Their political and social
beliefs were ultimately as widely divergent from those of Tone as were
their careers. So great was Tone's hatred of the law that he apparently
attended class on only three occasions. Most of his energy was devoted to
an almost obsessive round of theatre and opera. *Belmont Castle* was probably planned during the early days in London, but it was not completed
until the late summer of 1790.

It is possible to demonstrate from contemporary sources that many of
the fictitious characters in the book were based on people known at first
hand by one or all of the authors. The famous Mrs Delany substantiated
in her published diaries much of the petty gossip upon which they drew
so freely. The trio appear to have agreed on a system whereby Radcliffe
who was closely connected, by marriage, to both the Earl of Inchiquin
and Lord Charle-mont, would embellish his contribution by barely disguised references to known alliances, honourable and otherwise, within
the social precincts of these two families. Jebb, on the other hand, would

concentrate on the extravagances of a well-known dandy of the time, Sir Thomas Goold, and link the daughter of Inchiquin with his amorous pursuits. We know that Charlemont lavished praise on Goold, but the details of Goold's infatuation with Lady Cecilia in this novel are hilariously improbable and are no more than an indication of the spirit of fun that informs it. It is here, where Jebb departs from probability, that Tone's contribution matters most. With great skill and a delicious sense of irony, even malice, he uses the personae of Belville and Scudamore to compromise the reputation of Richard Martin and his wife Lady Elizabeth Vesey—with whom Tone had been in love years earlier—by elaborating a fiction for the understanding of which his audience needed few if any decoding skills. Tone created both the villain and the hero of the novel. Lord Mortimer may be regarded as the conventionally noble gentleman whose function is to restore normality when tragedy strikes. But both Belville and Scudamore are stronger, less stereotyped presences; they illustrate opposed aspects of Tone's personality and attitudes prior to his political development in the 1790s. At first reading, the authority of Tone's voice is disconcerting. It is only when the key to the novel is turned to unlock the plot's contemporary resonance that we recognize the indisputable authenticity and directness of Tone's contribution.

From his daily reading of *The Morning Post*, Tone gathered a store of miscellaneous information which he adroitly introduces into *Belmont Castle* for comic effect. His gaiety and his fondness for good wine and good food, his amusement at current fads and fashions such as the cult of sensibility and its attendant hypochondria, appear in the novel as characteristic features of a privileged and epicurean society. While particular and apposite references to persons or events connected with Lord Charlemont or with Murrough, the 5th Earl of Inchiquin, are detailed in the footnotes, it is proper to mention here the general range of social and cultural references he commanded. We learn the names of artists and performers who enjoyed the patronage of these illustrious families; we hear of the new gentlemen's clubs and the association between them and socially exclusive regiments of the army, such as the Coldstream Guards. Tone invokes technological innovations—the new German flute that could be broken up into sections, the new sulphur match—as well as the growing popularity of boxing matches, the welcome given to new institutions like hospitals and the current anxiety and hostility concerning conditions in prisons. In almost all instances the references are applicable to aspects of contemporary life in Dublin. This must have given his audience a pleasant shock of recognition.

The action takes place in London and its environs, but all the central characters are based on members of the Anglo-Irish ruling class or on people involved in Irish affairs. London is, in effect, a version of Dublin, and the patrician world of the two cities is represented here as the centre of high civilization. The growing distaste for the Grand Tour as a threat to native English morality is carried over into this novel in the opinions attributed to Mortimer, who avows himself relieved to have left behind the 'tinsel of French manners' and the licentiousness of the Italians and to have returned to the more austere morality of the British system, where chaste women were esteemed and cherished. Lord Charlemont was known throughout his life to have expressed distaste for the French.[6] Belville, modelled on William Ball, condemns the profligacy of young men who had travelled abroad. But the ostensible contrast between foreign licentiousness and native morality is treated ironically in *Belmont Castle*. Male characters pay lip-service to the exquisite sensibility and delicacy of maidens even as they themselves are having intrigues or affairs with 'sultanas' or 'married women' and plotting to violate the virginal innocence they pretend to admire. The wicked impulses may be 'foreign' but the double standards of the aristocratic playboy are native. This ironic element in the novel is of particular importance in the appreciation of the rather astonishing, even shameless, flamboyance of Tone's treatment of the spurious virtue of Georgiana, who is depicted as a chaste flirt, provoking in the villain's mind the very thoughts she is meant to abhor. Frequently the women who protest against intended assaults are presented as ambiguously weak and implausible in their denials.

Tone's declared intention was to write a burlesque of the prevailing sentimentalism of contemporary fiction. But this motive was replaced in time by a desire to exact retribution for a failed love affair with Lady Elizabeth Vesey during the years 1783–5. Much of the incidental material of the novel was gathered over the period 1788–90, and the scandal that supplied the central plot—Lady Vesey's elopement with a Mr Petrie— became public knowledge mere months before the publication of the novel. In order to humiliate a man whom he detested, Lady Vesey's husband Richard Martin, he was prepared to expose, in the most uninhibited manner, the wiles and absurdities of his own infatuation with Lady Vesey, the model for the disreputable wife of the story, Lady Elizabeth Clairville. *Belmont Castle* is, therefore, a curious document in which literary parody and caricature are used to expose a series of events well known to its intended readership. Before detailing this further, it is necessary to say something about the authors and the known history of the text.

THE HISTORY OF THE TEXT

When Tone was taken prisoner off the French warship *Hoche* at Buncrana, Co. Donegal, in 1798, two copies of *Belmont Castle* were among his confiscated effects. There was also a copy of *The Trial of Hurdy Gurdy*, a bitter parody on the savagery shown by the judiciary to the United Irishmen, written by William Sampson (whose daughter would one day marry Tone's son) and published in Belfast.[7] The third item confiscated was Tone's own *Address to the People of Ireland*, referred to in his journal of 1–2 November 1796: 'I have been hard at work … on an address to the people of Ireland, which is to be printed here [i.e. Brest] and distributed on our landing.'[8]

The bibliographer M.J. McManus has provided an authentic provenance for the two surviving copies of *Belmont Castle*. In 1939 McManus bought at an auction a copy of the book bearing the bookplate of John Boyd, the arresting sergeant in the militia that arrested Tone. This had been in Boyd's library since its confiscation (or, strictly speaking, its theft). With it were the copies of *The Trial of Hurdy Gurdy* and the *Address to the People of Ireland*, on the first of which was inscribed, 'I took these two off the *Hoche.*' The second surviving copy of *Belmont Castle* has a signature by Boyd that matches the handwriting in the sentence quoted. It somehow made its way (with no recorded intermediary) into the possession of the bibliographer E.R. McClintock Dix, who bequeathed it to the National Library of Ireland in 1935. This is the copy used in preparing the present edition.

Two pieces of information in the NLI copy of *Belmont Castle* proved invaluable in my research. Notes in pen by unknown hands describe Letter VII as a 'Portrait of T. G—d by R. J–bb' and Letter VIII as a 'Portrait of J.W. B—l by T.W. Tone'. This information was recorded by McManus, who produced a bibliography of Tone in 1940. On the basis of these clues and internal stylistic evidence, I sorted the letters into three groups. Tone's recognizable literary voice, which can be 'heard' in his autobiography and journals, was the main factor in the initial identification of his contributions. Scrutiny of the content of the letters allowed a further refinement of my attributions. Of the thirty-five letters that make up *Belmont Castle*, I attribute eighteen, or just over half the total, to Tone, ten to Radcliffe and seven to Jebb (see chart, p. vi).

At first I was primarily interested in identifying the authorial voice of

Tone. However, I kept wondering who T. G—d and J.W. B—l might be, and what bearing, if any, they might have on this work. I researched prominent figures of the period, and eventually determined that the character of Sir James Dashton was clearly modelled on Sir Thomas Goold, a well-known comtemporary of the authors. Further investigation revealed real-life models—some unmistakable, others more speculative—for the other characters in the novel and for the incidents described; these models are discussed below.

Founder and first president of the Bibliographical Society of Ireland in 1919, E.R. McClintock Dix (1857–1936) was an authority on the Dublin printers of the eighteenth century, and his research sheds light on the origins of this novel. A family of printers, James Byrne and his son Patrick, can be traced through their various premises in Dublin from 1749. Patrick seems to have had more than a professional acquaintance with Tone.[9] When Tone wrote his pamphlet advocating neutrality for Ireland in the war between Britain and revolutionary France, Byrne rejected it and was roundly cursed by Tone for his pains. Yet in 1790 Byrne was willing to risk the publication of *Belmont Castle*, in spite of the threat of libel that it posed. In November 1790 an unknown critic warned that 'despite the pleasure his pen affords us, our humane feelings should exert their monitory voice and check our transports'.[10] Many biographers of Tone thought this review a fake, a mere trick on the part of the authors to gain attention for a colourless novel; indeed, it is probable that the review was written by Tone himself. But the evidence indicates that there was good reason to encourage the exercise of a 'monitory voice' of 'our humane feelings': the risk of an action was real.

Byrne's shop, from 1784, was at 108 Grafton Street, near the house of Tone's in-laws and next door to the Irish Academy House, which was frequented by Tone. The Academy's membership included Lord Charlemont and William Ball, both of whom figure in the novel in disguised form. When Tone was a law student in the Temple in London, he reviewed regularly for Byrne's *Universal Magazine and Review*. His contributions, which I shall deal with in more detail below, were anonymous and are difficult to identify. But one can only wonder at the tenacity of a printer who offered Tone's later political pamphlets to the public and, according to one anecdote recorded by Tone, had to listen to denunciations from powerful figures such as Lord Cavendish, who once came into Byrne's bookshop to administer his rebukes while Tone hid behind the bookshelves. On Tone's last day in Dublin before going into exile in 1795, he was spotted by Lord Mountjoy in Byrne's shop.[11] Perhaps Byrne was indebted to

Tone for boosting sales of popular fiction through his reviews of novels
that he would have read in earlier London editions. But there was obviously a political bond between them as well. The *Hibernian Journal* for
April 1793 records that Byrne was fined £1000 and imprisoned for two
years for circulating Thomas Paine's *Common Sense.*

The fact that Tone had *Belmont Castle* with him on his fateful expedi-
tion to Lough Swilly might indicate that he had a special fondness for the
book and even for the life of a leisured man of letters which he had abandoned for separatist politics.[12] Yet the novel itself contains within it signs
of his ambivalent position in Anglo-Irish society. The letters written by
Tone expose that society's pervasive self-deception. Tone's intimacy with
the lives and loves of the gentry, as revealed in the novel, is countered by
the fact that the characters he introduced—Belville and Scudamore—are
also outsiders, men who do not quite belong to, though they are closely
involved with, that society. Belville, like Tone, has been 'contaminated by
trade';[13] he does not belong to the landed gentry, and Tone's presenta-
tion of him suggests that there is something contemptible and absurd in
the pretensions of the great and in efforts to gain entry into fashionable
society by submission to their principles. Belville is modelled on William
'Index' Ball, a man who embodied much of what Tone admired, while
Scudamore is unmistakably modelled on Tone himself, the raffish youth
of Trinity and the Inns of Court. Both characters are, in an important
sense, outsiders. Both die—one killed by a Lord in a swordfight, the other
by suicide. Had their love affairs been successful they would have gained
entry into Society, but that is not permitted them. Still smarting from the
after-effects of his affair with Lady Vesey, rendered more painful by the
public scandal of her new relationship, Tone seems to have seized the
opportunity to expose the hypocrisy and double standards of fashionable
society. His unease about his own position in this society is in marked contrast to the idealized versions of it given by his two co-authors, Radcliffe
and Jebb. This contrast is reflected in the different paths taken by the
three men after 1790. Tone became the most famous of Irish revolution-
aries while Radcliffe and Jebb became respected and increasingly conser-
vative members of the Anglo-Irish establishment.

RADCLIFFE

According to Francis O'Kelly, Radcliffe's name was not included in the
Catalogue of Eminent Middle Templars, even though by 1816 he had become

Judge of the Prerogative Court. O'Kelly implies that nothing else is known of him. This is not the case.

John Radcliffe's father had been a clergyman whose early death in 1766 may explain why, as an only child, he was moved at a tender age from Fermanagh to Drogheda. In his schooling there under Dr Norris he must have begun his life-long friendship with Richard Jebb. The senior members of these families were part of a wealthy philanthropic community in Dublin. This is worth noting because, in the novel, the penitent Scudamore is moved to make his final bequest to a hospital for 'poor, decayed and gouty men' (presumably Simpson's Hospital in Great Britain Street).[14] Radcliffe's father had two brothers who became judges, and it is likely that family precedent and perhaps family influence, as well as his own personal ambition and achievement, would have led him naturally in the same direction.[15]

Radcliffe's connections with the Charlemont and Inchiquin families, upon which he drew freely in his contributions to *Belmont Castle*, are bewilderingly complex and are best pursued through the intricacies of John Lodge's genealogy of Ireland.[16] It does seem that he had blood connections, albeit distant, with the leading aristocratic families. His mother's and his wife's relationships with the O'Briens, the Caulfeilds and the Watsons can be ascertained from an examination of several family pedigrees. These suffice to establish an intermarriage acquaintance with the most accomplished and prestigious of the figures who appear thinly disguised in the novel and to validate the claim he makes in his editorial address that he had at least a glimpse of his illustrious audience in domestic retirement.

In 1787 Radcliffe married Catherine Cox. Her father, the Rev. Michael Cox, Archbishop of Cashel, had previously been married to Ann O'Brien, cousin of Murrough, the 5th Earl of Inchiquin. Her brother, Sir Richard Eyre Cox, was connected to the same family by his marriage (c.1784) to Maria O'Brien, the niece of Inchiquin. Her grandfather, Sir Richard Cox, 'a most intelligent, well-informed gentleman', was recommended by Charlemont for his 'correspondence in 1878 with Sir Lucius O'Brien, in which he displays a perfect intimacy with Irish affairs'.[17] Radcliffe's own mother was the daughter of Robert Mason, who was a direct descendant of the Watson line of the Marquis of Rockingham's family.

When Catherine's stepmother died in childbirth, Mrs Delany commented that she was 'much lamented by everyone'.[18] Catherine's cousin, John Eyre Cox, had a daughter, Mary, who married Francis Caulfeild, brother to Lord Charlemont. The tragic circumstances of this family's death is one of the first and strongest of the novel's indisputable references to Charlemont. His brother left London on 9 November 1775 to take his place in the Irish Senate. He was accompanied by his wife and daughter and an 'infant 3 years old'. They all perished in a storm outside Dublin; their ship appears to have gone down at Parkgate while coming up the river to the port.[19]

This three-year-old is resurrected in the novel as the orphan Juliana, the beloved of Mortimer. Mortimer is himself an idealized portrait of all that is best in the family history of the Caulfeilds and the O'Briens. His marriage to Juliana, which breaks the family's traditional opposition to marriage to anyone socially inferior, possibly owes something to the well-known sponsorship by Sir Lucius O'Brien of Charlemont's own marriage to Mary Hickman, whose sister Charlotte had married Edward, the brother of Sir Lucius.[20]

Mortimer's name, career and ancestry are based on those of Murrough, the 5th Earl of Inchiquin. Both find it necessary to adjust to the unexpected acquisition of great wealth. However, Mortimer's literary tastes and his hostility to the seductions of foreign travel reproduce the recorded opinions of Charlemont. Radcliffe paints the latter and the 'good old Earl'—the 4th Earl of Inchiquin—as virtually without fault. Only the merest trace of a fashionable sensibility detracts from Mortimer's characteristic steadiness and good sense.

When Juliana describes the decor of her London home, the detail is remarkably similar to Mrs Delany's description of her arrangement of books, her china and the chenille work on her chairs at Delville. Lord John's (i.e. Charlemont's) house in Grosvenor Square has an 'ante-chamber hung with delicate silk, the chairs matching the hangings with a delicate lilac silk ... finest porcelain ... and a book-case stored with our choicest English china'. The variety of 'spruce villas, humble cottages, rich woods, smooth lawns, lofty towers and glittering spires' that delights Juliana's eye is suggestive of the features that diversified Charlemont's demesne at Marino.[21] Juliana, whose surname is Blandford, is introduced by Radcliffe with an apology for the 'very imperfect' story he has of her.[22]

Tone praised the letters written by Radcliffe in *Belmont Castle* as 'far the best'.[23] This is debatable. Certainly Radcliffe had a flair and elegance that transformed the fairly mundane material with which he had to deal, along with a certain skill and grace in disguising his borrowings. There is a pertinent anecdote about his grandfather, Stephen Radcliffe, Vicar of Naas, who had been at the centre of a row for having dared to criticize a lecture given by Dr Edward Synge on 'The toleration of Popery', delivered at St Patrick's Cathedral. What is of interest here is not the argument itself but rather the vitriolic abuse that Stephen Radcliffe's writings received from Synge, who attacked them as 'senseless, dull, insipid and ill-natured'. Apparently his adaptation of quotations from Spenser's *The Faerie Queene* (Book I, Canto IX, Stanza 43) were so 'altered in expression and sentiment' that one could 'scarce know it in disguise'.[24] John Radcliffe may have imitated his grandfather's technique of the interwoven quotation from established authors, but he was certainly more subtle and successful in his use of it.

JEBB

Richard Jebb's grandfather settled as a merchant in Drogheda in the early part of the eighteenth century. Sir Richard Jebb, physician to George III and first cousin of Ann Radcliffe, the famous Gothic novelist, was a nephew of the grandfather. As he did not marry, he donated his considerable fortune to his favourite uncle's grandson—that is, to Richard, the co-author of *Belmont Castle*. Richard's younger brother, John, became the Bishop of Limerick in 1823. It is from John and from John's biographer that we learn much of what is known about Richard, to whose generosity John 'owed his education, his rank in society and himself'.[25] Richard, who was educated at the endowed school of Drogheda, acted as guardian to John after the death of their mother. He spent a number of years in France with his uncle after leaving Trinity College, where he was a class fellow. By 1788 he was back in Ireland again, arranging for John to move from school at Celbridge to Derry. Between December 1790 and July 1791, in the interval between school and college, John resided with his brother. At the time Richard strove to coax John into taking up the army as a profession, proposing that he raise a company in a new regiment. These particulars coincide with the histories of Mortimer and Dashton in *Belmont Castle*: having inherited a massive fortune from an uncle in the wake of a family death, Mortimer had, like Richard, just returned from France; and Dashton, like John, was under considerable pressure to take up the army as a career. But John Jebb decided upon the Church, and thrived, contrary to Richard's fear that he would 'live and die a curate'.[26]

In the early 1790s Tone recommended Richard Jebb to the Dissenters at Drogheda as a barrister able to defend them. As the decade progressed, Tone's and Jebb's political views evolved in opposite directions. In 1799

Jebb published *A Reply to a Pamphlet entitled, Arguments for and against the Union*. This pamphlet, in which he argued forcefully, on economic grounds, against the legislative union of Britain and Ireland, made a great impression. The removal from Ireland of 'five and twenty of the principal nobility' or of 'eighty or ninety of the first gentlemen',[27] he argued, would be economically disastrous. He defended the legal profession for its cool and patriotic wisdom and behaviour during the recent crisis. As for the Catholics: 'Let them publicly declare that to an Irish Parliament only [i.e. a Protestant one] will they be indebted for their full and complete advance to the privileges and honours of the constitution.'[28] The *DNB* describes Jebb as an 'impartial' judge, but it is not easy to reconcile this description with the attitude of one who agreed with the parliament's opinion that 'the cause of our dangers and our troubles [is] a conspiracy of Republicanism, working upon the vices, the prejudices of a poor uninstructed people'.[29]

Jebb displays symptoms of the shock his class had experienced as a result of the 1798 rebellion. The disputes for and against the Union had, in his view, 'abetted the progress and circumstances of the Rebellion'.[30] He was alert to the passions of Orangemen and of rebels, recognizing that both were agitated and distracted at the close of the uprising. He understood that the accusation that the Catholics were trying to reduce the Protestants to a 'state of nullity' did not sufficiently allow for the distinction between Catholic and republican. Not all Catholics were republicans and certainly not all republicans were Catholics. Even so, Jebb went on in his next publication, *A Letter of Remonstrance to Denys Scully Esq. upon his Advice to his Catholic brethren, by an Irish Loyalist* (1803), to support and praise parliament for its 'laudable diligence' and single-mindedness in setting out to suppress the 'barbarous satisfaction'[31] of the Catholics. He expresses indignation that Scully, a barrister who was later to achieve fame with his *Statement of the Penal Laws* (1812), should misrepresent as 'wanton and barbarous cruelty'[32] the disciplined action of the military in putting down the 1798 rebellion. Jebb argues that Scully should not try to equate the 'necessary example of punishment upon traitors' with the 'merciless murders, committed by furious bigots, upon unarmed, unoffending gentlemen, whose only crime was loyalty to their King'.[33] He defends the loyalty of Orangemen, although he 'belongs not to their body'—for he condemns all party distinctions. Further, he declares that 'no class of man and no individual, but United Irishmen, are clamorous'.[34] Once again he notes that 'neglect of education' has 'made them the ready instrument of rebellion' and hopes that 'an ever-watchful government may provide protection and support to the Gentry of Ireland as shall render their abodes and estates secure and delightful'.[35]

Shortly after the Act of Union, a seat in the imperial parliament was offered to Jebb by the government he had opposed. He declined the offer, and he could not subsequently be induced to stand for his native city of Drogheda, even though he would certainly have been returned. Jebb's increasing faith and reliance in law and order led him in time to the positions of third, then second sergeant-at-law in Drogheda and eventually to the position of fourth Justice of the Irish Court of King's bench in 1818. In his *The Freedom of the Press in Ireland*, Brian Inglis describes Jebb's notoriety as a judge as on a par with that of Lord Norbury. Jebb continued to identify justice with the interests of his own class and began to show a marked partiality for the Orange Order. In defiance of normal judicial practice, he chose his own part of the country for his circuit, but 'not content with that outrage, he had chosen out of that respectable district, three most questionable names for Sheriffs—the first two being the proposer and seconder of his son's election'. Inglis quotes an accusation that, while Jebb remained in power, a 'newspaper could not hope for a fair trial', so rigorous was his censorship.[36]

In 1799, the year of Jebb's renowned *Reply*, another of his Trinity contemporaries became involved in the war of words over the Union. He was Sir Thomas Goold, the model for Sir James Dashton in *Belmont Castle*. Goold had gained notoriety shortly after his return from France in 1790 when he issued a pamphlet answering the various attacks on Edmund Burke by such opponents as Joseph Towers, Richard Price and Joseph Priestley.[37] A flamboyant figure, he had captured the limelight as a self-proclaimed expert on almost any subject. He had chosen a career in law merely as a step towards much higher things. Details of Goold's dress, acrobatic feats and general reputation for exotic appearance and quixotic behaviour are documented in William Curran's *Sketches of the Irish Bar* (2 vols, 1885). The name Dashton was derived from his possession of

… an imposing phaeton, in which Kitty Cut-a-Dash of fascinating memory, and then reigning illegitimate belle of Dublin, by his side, he scoured through streets and squares with the brilliancy and rapidity of a meteoric coruscation.[38]

Curran recalls with incredulity how Goold, 'flaming in a pink satin jockey-dress, distanced every competitor and bore away the Curragh Cup'. He depicts a dandy dressed in 'bright and various tints' who was preoccupied with wealth and pleasure, and who 'played, sang, danced and rode with skill and spirit'.[39] In Radcliffe's version of him as Sir James Dashton, the same elements remain—he 'leaped over the heads' of the domestics in his pursuit of Juliana[40]—but they are altered by the ultimate emergence from this playboy chrysalis of a mature and likeable adult of great energy and learning. Radcliffe scarcely exaggerates in his description of Dashton's dress:

His coat was of a pale rose-coloured satin, lined with the most delicate blue; his cape and cuffs like the lining, richly embroidered with silver, his waistcoat white tissue, trimmed with sable, his shoes of black satin with red heels and tied with bunches of pink ribbon intermixed with silver foil.[41]

Jebb, on the other hand, emphasizes the irresponsible features of Dashton's personality. His Dashton is capable of blunt sexual language,[42] as in his verse on Georgiana's rescue from a charging ram, in letter XV:

> Sweet briar wounds—the rose has thorns
> And eke, alas! the Ram has horns;
> But this huge Ram had been a boar
> If Georgiana he should gore.

Goold's talents were displayed in his pamphlet *An Address to the People of Ireland on the Subject of the Projected Union* (1799). In a fiercely indignant spirit and with a display of great rhetorical skill, he condemned the excesses of British policy on the question of the Union. He supported his anti-Union position with an impressive display of arguments informed by his wide knowledge of foreign policy, the state of Irish trade, commerce, manufacture and national debt. At the centre of his argument we find an impassioned outburst against the superstition and bigotry of the Orangemen, counterbalanced by a heartfelt plea to Catholics to renounce their policy of 'extermination'. He condemns the 'diabolical' purpose of the British militia and laments what he called the 'Calends of May, 1798 [which] were written in blood'.[43] Finally, he denounces the notion of Empire as 'sacrilegious' and commends the policy of the Irish Volunteers, regretting that there is not 'another Charlemont to plead the cause for Ireland'.[44]

Despite his opposition to the Union and to British policy in Ireland, Goold was no radical; like Jebb, he eventually became sergeant-at-law in Drogheda, before attaining the position of master of the Court of Chancery.[45] It angered him that anyone opposed to the Union was 'branded' as a French Republican or United Irishman.[46] He was, in fact, a characteristic 'patriot' of the eighteenth century, loyal to a conception of Ireland that was not incompatible with an admiration for the recent achievements of the Protestant ruling class, its 'sumptuous mansions' and 'stately edifices' and the 'degree of enviable splendour'[47] that it had attained. Lord Charlemont was the most characteristic representative of all that Goold admired in Ireland's recent political and architectural revival.

A further correlation between *Belmont Castle* and contemporary fact is provided in the character of Colonel Watworth, a correspondent of Dashton's, who is based on Charles Watson Wentworth (1730–82). Wentworth, who inherited vast wealth and property as well as his father's title of Marquis of Rockingham, had become head of the Treasury under Pitt in 1765. The latter, who disliked Wentworth, was accused by Edmund Burke of having 'bullied' Wentworth into a repeal of the Stamp Act in that year. We are told that Pitt 'took the earliest opportunity of testifying his disapprobation' of Wentworth's appointment.[48] Thus the significance of Dashton's remark, 'No, Watworth, wait till the next session, and if I don't annoy Pitt ...'[49]

Besides the political background, Wentworth (who was not a contemporary of Goold's) has in common with Dashton and the Watworth of the novel a preoccupation with the breeding and racing of horses, a characteristic avocation of the Anglo-Irish gentry. The connection with Burke was further enhanced by Wentworth's friendship with Lord Charlemont, who erected a monument to his memory after his death, and by Goold's reference in his 1799 pamphlet to meeting the representative of Rockingham at Burke's house. But the connection between Watworth and Dashton in the novel is useful also in highlighting for us the difference in treatment accorded to Dashton by Radcliffe and Jebb. Radcliffe gives the soft, Jebb the harsh version of the young man's character, and the connection with Watworth, most especially in the references to his accomplishment and extravagance with horses, provides the authors with the opportunity to give the portrait their own peculiar emphases.

WILLIAM BALL

The character of Belville in *Belmont Castle*, created by Tone, is modelled on William 'Index' Ball (1749–1828) of Dublin. Like Belville, William Ball was the 'younger branch of an ancient family'.[50] Tone plays mockingly on the young man's repeated complaint about his lack of fortune and noble birth. William's father, the Rev. Thomas Ball, was Master of the Classical School in St. Michael le Pole's at Great Ship Street, Dublin. Many noted figures passed through the school during his mastership, including Henry Grattan, John Fitzgibbon and Sir Jonah Barrington. Barrington was bitter in his comments on the education he received there:

I was required to learn English Grammar in the Latin tongue: and to translate languages without understanding any of them. I was taught prosody without verse and rhetoric without composition; and before I ever heard of an oration, I was flogged for not minding my emphasis on recitation.[51]

Rev. Ball seems to have had a very tenuous position in the school. After many years' service, he had to resort to a petition for a permanent post and was given permission by an Act of Vestry to 'teach the languages in the said house during his continuance in the Parish, provided it be applied to that use and no other'.[52] He had become an object of charity, despite his scholarly background. His son John temporarily halted the decline in the school's fortunes. However, by 1787 it was used by St Bride's Vestry for almshouses. (In *Belmont Castle*, the dying and penitent Scudamore wills donations to local almshouses.)

Both sons, William and John, followed their father's literary pursuits, although Tone implies that William's capacities in this regard were limited. John helped with some researches in St Patrick's Cathedral and was chaplain to the Dowager Countess of Barrymore. He wrote ballads, odes and elegies which were published in Dublin in 1772. In 1782 he set up the Lyceum in Great Ship Street to 'cultivate a taste for the liberal arts, to accommodate such as wish to pursue their studies in private: or to complete the education of a gentleman'.[53] It is difficult to say whether the project was primarily educational or commercial. The building, opened by the Archbishop of Dublin, was fitted up with 'a variety of Apartments, and provided with proper masters and assistants to qualify for civil, military, naval and mercantile affairs; and students are prepared for the university'.[54] John also produced a volume of poems, *Fading Leaves*, and contributed to *Walker's Hibernian Magazine*.[55] He died in reduced circumstances in Longford Street in 1812. One of his pupils during the 1780s had been Radcliffe's cousin, John, from whom the co-authors may have received information on the vagaries of the institution's fortunes.

The various and snide references to the Ball family by Tone in *Belmont Castle* indicate that they had attracted his attention. William succeeded in fascinating him. The two men had similar backgrounds, training and education. Both were convivial and public-spirited members of the professional middle class, hovering rather uneasily on the verges of aristocratic Anglo-Irish society. At Trinity both had had distinguished careers. Ball received a foundation scholarship in 1767, and was a member of the Historical Society, to which he gave the opening address in 1775. Tone, as auditor of the Society, gave the closing address in 1786. The Society had a body of codified regulations and its meetings included a history examination, a debate and the submission of essays and poems. Medals were awarded, and subscriptions were collected for the relief of the poor. John Hely-Hutchinson, who opened the university to Catholics, frequented the society in Ball's time. As the Volunteer movement grew in strength, politics became an increasing preoccupation. In the first debate on Irish political matters in 1779, the Society rejected the proposal of the Union. As the political atmosphere intensified in the eighties, Tone took the Society to task for being a 'Theatre of war and Tumult'.[56] In 1798 it carried a motion against its former auditor and adjourned until the rebellion ended.

William Ball was the first treasurer of the Royal Irish Academy, whose earliest meetings were held at the Dublin town house of Lord Charlemont in Rutland Square. The Academy's membership in its inaugural year of 1785 comprised thirty-eight of the most eminent and erudite men of the day, including four fellows of Trinity. Ball was one of the first contributors to the compulsory essays read by the learned members in the first month, on the subject of 'The Process of the Mind in Abstraction'. Another of the founder members, Mathew Young, was Tone's first tutor at Trinity.

Ball was primarily known as the compiler of the *Index to the Statutes at Large, Passed in the Parliament Held in Ireland*, from which he gained his nickname. This mammoth enterprise engaged him for over eight years until its publication in 1799.[57] In the *Index*, Ball painstakingly documented records of the Statutes; he received a state grant of £5000 towards their publication. Legal, military and mercantile affairs are catalogued, ranging from the duty on tobacco to the accommodation assigned to judges, from revenue and import taxes to a register of the publications of the King's Inns. In the entry on the '98 Rebellion, he conscientiously lists 'Juries finding verdicts, against oficers who ... in suppressing rebellion, act maliciously'.[58]

This notable if rather pedantic aspect of Ball's achievement forms a contrast with the issues and themes that engaged him as a poet. In 1789 he translated Jean-Baptiste-Louis Gresset's comic poem about a parrot that, in its passage between two convents, picks up the language of the sailors who transported it. *Vert-Vert* might seem an incongruous project for the compiler of the great *Index*, but his own poems, which appeared in Joshua Edkin's *Collection of Poems* (2 vols, Dublin, 1789–90), confirm the impression given by the translation of a gift for light or sentimental verse with a decided preference for the comic or burlesque. In a poem on how to seduce a lady, for instance, using the image of a nettle, he advises that a man should

> Grasp it strongly round
> And pluck it boldly from the ground

lest

> touched with caution or with fear
> It wounds the flesh and draws a tear. [59]

He also shared with Tone a profound dislike for the profession of the law. But whereas Tone abandoned it, Ball resigned himself to it, however dismal the prospect.

> Condemned in the lead mines of law books to dig,
> And refine the rich ore, 'til it shines like a pig,
> To leave all the Fine Arts ... for statutes at large.[60]

This reference to his *Index of Statutes* then leads him to declaim:

> Say Muses! how first the difference arose
> Or how the law and poetry came to be foes.

The poetry of Belville in the novel, except where it is imitative of Shenstone, is bathetic. It is a traditional mixture of sentimentality, bawdiness and Gothic extravagance, although Tone has a much greater sense of irony than Ball. But, no doubt, the poems, like the novel, were 'most relished by the author and his immediate connections'.[61] For Tone these connections would have included Ball, and in creating Belville Tone seems to have found a means of presenting, in a kindly light, the fusion of pedantry and sentimental humour that was a feature of Ball's personality.

In the novel, Belville takes a farm adjacent to Belmont Castle—based on Charlemont's estate at Marino—in order to be close to his beloved. Rocque's map of 1777[62] shows that Charlemont's property was immediately adjacent to that of the Balls of Moorside, and some of the most memorable events and trysts in the book take place at the Moor, the Forest and the Grove, all marked on the map as features of the two estates.

The 'too amiable Belville' encroaches upon the affections of the Shirley family as if 'by chance alone'.[63] When Georgiana in all innocence declares 'that he may not be what he seems', and on her deathbed wishes Mortimer to attend to the needs of the young man who had 'become intimate with the family', it is hard to escape the analogy between this story and that of Ball's pursuit of influential connections with the O'Brien family, particularly Sir Lucius and the Earl of Charlemont, founder-members, like him, of the Royal Irish Academy. However, it is equally true that Belville may represent, in a mocking fashion, what Tone believed he himself might have become had he remained within the confines of the literary-professional world of his class and time.[64] This mockingly benign version of himself is, however, countered by the more disobliging version represented by Scudamore and his relationship with Lady Clairville. To the background of this relationship we now turn.

TONE, SCUDAMORE AND THE VESEY AFFAIR

In the letters attributed to Scudamore, Tone's style is noticeably freer, livelier and less inhibited than in the Ball/Belville episodes. There is a decidedly histrionic flavour to the portrayal and a more straightforwardly comic exploitation of the material. The intricate plot involving Scudamore, Colonel Neville, Lady Middleton and Lady Clairville is an amalgam of contemporary facts, sometimes distorted for reasons that may have more to do with discretion than valour; but there is also in Tone's version of contemporary happenings a readiness to ridicule. The name of Tone's counterpart in the novel, Fitzroy Scudamore, derives from the case of Lady Frances Scudamore, who after the death of her husband in 1741 married her lover, Charles Fitzroy. Without losing his reputation for loose living, Fitzroy managed through this marriage to gain great wealth and to inherit the title of Duke Scudamore. Colonel Neville, the character in the novel who provides Fitzroy Scudamore with friendship, advice and support in his sexual escapades, was sufficiently recognizable to provoke a reviewer of the novel to rebuke the authors for their harshness in treating this gentleman 'late of the Coldstream Guards'.[65] The hilarious if rather gruesome details of the duel between Lord Clairville and Scudamore is almost certainly a mocking account of the proposed duel in London between the actual Lieutenant Colonel Neville and the Duke of York, who had slighted the Colonel at a masque. (In the novel, a masque also provides a rendezvous for the adulterous lovers and is a prelude to the duel.)

The Duke of York refused the challenge, and on 30 May 1787 the following statement was issued:

It is the opinion of His Majesty's Coldstream Regiment of Guards that Lieutenant
Neville, subsequent to the 15th instant, has behaved with courage, but, from the
peculiarity of circumstances, not with judgement.[66]

   The particulars of these scattered events were taken up by Tone, Jebb
and Radcliffe and blended with an unusual tale recounted in the
Autobiography and Correspondence of Mrs Delany, the famous Mary
Granville (1700–88). There we hear of a Mr Middleton, a young gentleman of no fortune, brother to the Irish Lord Middleton, who fell in love
with a young woman of no birth or fortune. Through the intervention of
Lord Clair, the young man was forced to give up his proposed marriage,
as a consequence of which his beloved 'fell into a consumption'[67] and
died. On hearing this, the young man contracted a fever and died within a few days. In the novel, the names Middleton and Clair(ville) are
retained—though the latter may have been more directly inspired by the
name of Richard Martin's house, Clareville—and the resemblance
between the stories of Juliana and Mortimer and of Georgiana and
Belville and the account given by Mrs Delany was sufficiently obvious.
The conflict between the demands of passion and the obligations of society is, of course, a standard one in novels of this kind. When Scudamore
discovers that his steward 'had a daughter whom he was pleased to represent as not totally unworthy of becoming my sultana for the present',[68]
we hear an echo of the young woman's father in Mrs Delany's story
telling Mr Middleton that her birth made her 'much too low to be his
wife, and much above being his mistress'.[69] In a similar vein, Juliana
would rather perish than disappoint the high hopes of Mortimer's father,
who expected his son to marry someone of his own class. The French
woman in Mrs Delany's account also tried to persuade Mr Middleton out
of his desire to marry her and thereby disappoint his family's hopes.
Lord Clair's interference in writing to Mr Middleton's relations to
acquaint them of his amour is duplicated in the novel, along with the
ultimately tragic consequences of the death of the two young lovers.
   While Jebb and Radcliffe worked this incident into the plot of the
novel, Tone went much further by including a version of his early love
affair with Lady Elizabeth Vesey of Lucan, and of Lady Vesey's notorious
affair with one Mr Petrie, which became the subject of widespread gossip in 1790—'at a date recent indeed', as the Editor of *Bemont Castle*
writes.[70]

Tone's candour in his portrayal of Scudamore and the relationship with Lady Clairville is of itself the strongest evidence that this novel is in part a glamorization by Tone of his dissipated and much-enjoyed youth. During the year 1782 Tone had stayed for long periods in the home of Lady Vesey and her husband Richard Martin (1754–1834), where he was employed to teach Martin's two half-brothers. He used this as an opportunity to rehearse the various parts which, as an amateur actor, he played in the theatrical entertainments Lady Vesey favoured.[71] So the young Tone at once 'gratified his passion for music and silently advanced his suit with her ladyship'[72] during a period when 'urgent business' had drawn Richard Martin, an MP, to London, whence he was not to return for three days—'to my delight, three ages'.[73] Tone's willingness to ridicule Lady Vesey and her husband may be explained by the coquetry with which she had teased him in earlier days. In his autobiography he records:

As I preserved, as well as felt the proudest respect for her, she supposed she might amuse herself innocently in observing the progress of this terrible passion in the mind of an interesting young man of twenty: but this is an experiment no woman ought to make.[74]

Only readers of *Belmont Castle* can estimate how Tone redressed the balance. He did this largely through references not to his own (generally unknown) infatuation with Lady Vesey, but to the news of Lady Vesey's elopement with Petrie in 1790, shortly before the publication of *Belmont Castle*. Lady Vesey deserted Richard Martin in a manner and in circumstances coincident with those surrounding the escapades of Scudamore and Belville in *Belmont Castle*. Although names are transposed here and there, the relationship between the actual and the fictional events is beyond question and the attempts to disguise it are desultory in the extreme.

The famous elopement is reproduced in various details in the novel. As Shevawn Lynam tells us in *Humanity Dick: A Biography of Richard Martin M.P.* (London, 1975), Mr Petrie, Lady Vesey's new lover, wrote to her instructing her to hire a coach which would take her from her brother's house in Clarges Street to the Adelphi. On the way, she was to disguise herself by changing her clothes and rubbing burnt cork on her eyebrows and rouge on her cheeks. Her unsuspecting husband had bidden her farewell and was returning to France via Dover when news that the Irish Parliament had dissolved caused him to forgo his business arrangements and return home. She made plausible excuses and he had no reason then to suspect that he was being cuckolded. It was only when she settled down to live openly in Soho Square that he began to speculate and finally to act. One of the apocryphal tales surrounding him tells of his dressing as an Eastern pedlar (although not quite 'wrapped in a black domino', as in the novel) [75] to gain admission to the house where his wife was staying. 'There he found her in the arms of Petrie who almost died of shock, assuming that he was about to be challenged to a duel by the man who had earned himself the nickname of "Hair-Trigger Dick".' [76]

Scudamore's death at the hands of the outraged husband is a comic exaggeration of what happened to Petrie, who escaped unharmed and unchallenged. Instead, Richard Martin, imputing his wife's action to a 'deranged mind', [77] took a criminal conversation action against Petrie and won it. *The Freeman's Journal* published a report that cast doubt on the legitimacy of Martin's children, a matter of significance for Tone as well as for Martin, since Tone's affair had been succeeded by Lady Vesey's pregnancy. Besides, Tone did not agree with the verdict in Martin's favour. He felt that Martin had treated his wife with characteristic neglect and he wrote in his autobiography: 'I am satisfied from my own observations and knowledge of the characters of both parties during my residence for many months in their family, that the fault was originally Martin's.' [78]

It is difficult to decide just how far Tone was indulging in a personal vendetta and how far he was simply having fun at the expense of the Martins. Some of the scenes appear at first to be harmless comic parodies of the disappointed lover or lovers in their usual stereotyped roles. The spectacle of Scudamore coming down to breakfast 'with only one stocking on, and without my *Robe de chambre*' and absentmindedly pouring 'coffee into the sugar bowl' [79] is one typical example. It seems to be one of a number of episodes in which the absurdity of the sentimental lover is emphasized. Lady Clairville, holding 'her ivory finger on the spring of the bell' while Scudamore threatens a suicide which she thinks it gross of him to dare commit 'in her presence', [80] provides another instance, as does Scudamore immediately afterwards when he rushes home in ecstasy and collides on the way with a chimney-sweep with whom he becomes involved in a long and complicated imbroglio, well calculated to dampen any passion. The 'gross sensuality' of 'boiled chicken' and a 'flask of Burgundy' [81] can also console the passionate Scudamore in his despair, and the lady's conventional pretensions to unsullied purity and innocence can appear suspect when her protestations carry an explicit sexual innuendo: '... draw thy bright sword ... and sheathe it in this bosom while it is yet spotless'. [82] Scudamore is attractive because he is refreshingly honest about his aims. He becomes increasingly candid in his letters to Colonel Neville about the pleasures an illicit affair affords him, and he manages to preserve, in all his difficulties, a sense of humour which is a tonic change from the simpering pieties and goodness of more conventionally moral people like Juliana, Belville and Mortimer. So, at one level, we are inclined to congratulate the authors on having successfully 'scribbled a volume'.[83] Yet, when we look again, and see reproduced in many of these instances episodes and verbatim phrases from the play *The Fair Penitent* by Nicholas Rowe, in which Martin and Lady Vesey had given many virtuoso performances, the comedy loses some of its cheerful innocence and we see again how directly Tone was attacking a couple already undergoing a painful public exposure of their private lives.[84] On a number of occasions, the stylized and histrionic language has such palpable sexual overtones that Tone seems to be using his undoubted literary skills to inflict as much pain as possible on the unfortunate pair. But the Vesey affair or affairs certainly give to the novel an interest and appeal that distinguish it from the many other novels of the period in which the excesses of sentimentalism had been mocked.

LITERARY BACKGROUNDS TO THE NOVEL

The most obvious literary presences in the novel, most of them invoked by Tone, are Shakespeare, Shenstone and Goethe. Shakespeare is the most prevalent of these, not only in direct quotations, but in a deliberately designed imitation of what Marilyn Butler has called 'the heightened passions ... and stylized poetic techniques of the Elizabethan dramatists',[85] which had been introduced by Horace Walpole in *The Castle of Otranto* (1765) and was characteristic of the Shakespearean revival pioneered on the stage by Garrick. Tone's language is haunted by Shakespearean echoes, most of them having their source in the great tragedies. The effect here is parodic, since he was using the implied grandeur of his model to emphasize the absurdity of the sentimental story he is telling.

Shenstone is cited frequently to emphasize the pastoral quality of Belville's retreat, and the rather artificial prettiness for which Shenstone has been much criticized is entirely in keeping with this aspect of the work's satirical intent. Belville on his farm is meant to remind us of Shenstone on his estate at Leasowes—a model for Charlemont's demesne at Marino—and his general attitude is comparable to that expressed in

Shenstone's best-known poem, the 'Pastoral Ballad' of 1755. Tone was, therefore, both following and making fun of current practice in providing a literary background that would give added resonance as well as a sharper point to his novel's curious mixture of tragic, pastoral and satiric motifs.

In the case of Goethe's *The Sorrows of Young Werther* (1780–1), Tone was unambiguously ironic in his adaptation of the famous original to the episode in which Belville commits suicide. In this passage, he openly takes phrases from Goethe. Belville drinks more wine than usual and contemplates the great metaphysical problems of annihilation and 'dissolution' before discharging some 'trifling debts' and bidding 'adieu' to his mistress. Tone exploits the discrepancy between Werther's and Belville's situation in order to remind us of the inanity of the world (and of the novel) that Belville inhabits. So he takes, verbatim, the passage in which Werther declares that 'good Christians will not chuse that their bodies should be interred near the unhappy corpse of an unhappy miserable wretch like me', and preserves its satiric application while simultaneously allowing us to see how comically out of proportion the tragic note is in this instance. The farewells that echo as 'the clock strikes twelve'[86] may have wrung tears from Goethe's readers or from avid sentimentalists in 1790, but must have created great amusement for those attuned to the origins of Belville in Ball and Tone and the distance between *Belmont Castle's* mock grief and the *Weltschmerz* of its German model.

Tone, as we have seen, was no stranger to the contemporary novel. His three years as a reviewer coincided with the emergence, in the late 1770s, of the patriotic novels which insisted on making the settings of their stories Irish, in however nominal a fashion. Thus in *The Fair Hibernian*, reviewed in *The European Magazine* during Tone's stint as a writer for it, the heroine, Valerie O'Brien, daughter of an 'Irish baronet', insists on her French lover living in Ireland and on her French friends changing the misnomer 'La Belle Anglaise' to 'La Belle Irlandaise'.[87] The French flavour was not accidental, and was indeed to survive into the novels of Lady Morgan in the early nineteenth century, when the 'national novel' would come into its own. *The Dublin Town and Country Magazine* of March 1785 provided a recipe for such novels in an article entitled 'Every Man His Own Novelist', recommending that 'simplicity' should be avoided as much as possible and making French 'de rigeur'. Lady Morgan certainly followed the magazine's advice in both cases, as did *Belmont Castle*, although Tone and his coauthors did so for comic effect. It is possible that Tone reviewed *The Fair Hibernian*; it gained an anonymous notice in *The European Magazine* in February 1790 and this was reproduced in Byrne's *Universal Magazine*.

INTRODUCTION

We can be much more certain about another source novel, *Emmeline: The Orphan and the Castle*, by Charlotte Smith, reviewed in November 1788 in *The London Review*. It is the subject of a heated debate in a Letter of *Belmont Castle* between a Major Welton and Belville. The absurd creation of 'demi-gods in lace coats and goddesses in satin' for which the Major denounces novels is virtually a caricature of Radcliffe's portrayal of Belville, who defends novels in this dispute. Further, the Major's claim that a 'novelist would blindfold our judgement while he inflames our imagination'[88] is a marked echo of the reviewer, the 'unknown critic', who wrote: 'The generality of our novels are calculated to inflame the passions and deprave our understanding.' The reviewer goes on to claim that this particular novel is superior in that it 'successfully endeavoured to instruct the mind and improve the heart'.[89] Belville characterizes this novel as a 'most elegant and refined amusement'.[90] In this interpolated episode, we may well be witnessing the author, Radcliffe, teasing Tone about his expressed views on novels and on Charlotte Smith's work, as they had appeared in the review.

CONCLUSION

Belmont Castle is a parody of the sentimental novel and a satire upon the inanity and venality of the society to which its authors belonged. But it is also a light-hearted literary squib, written by three law students who decided to avail of some of the opportunities presented by contemporary affairs to write a *roman-à-clef*, perhaps to see to what extent it would be accurately decoded and appreciated.

Tone's contribution, especially in relation to the Lady Vesey affairs, seems to have scandalized few or none. He was, of course, exposing his own reputation to obloquy as well as those of Lady Vesey and Dick Martin. He seemed unable to resist the opportunity that Lady Vesey's sensational affair with Petrie threw open to him; perhaps he was glad to take the chance to relieve himself of an obsession. Only those already in the know could take pleasure in the exposure, but today's reader needs an almost blow-by-blow account to appreciate the force of Tone's semi-humorous and yet bitter assault. This is clearly one of the reasons for the novel's falling into almost total obscurity, but the inner circle of readers who could appreciate it may have allowed it to disappear from sight because the most prominent of its authors had blotted his copybook in other ways. His suicide, unlike that of Belville, could not be smiled away.

A NOTE ON THE TEXT

For this edition of *Belmont Castle* I have retained the original spellings, but in the interest of clarity I have made some minor alterations in punctuation. The heavy use of dashes and exclamation marks was a convention of the epistolary novel, conveying immediacy and adding to the emotional excess which is the hallmark of the novel of sensibility; to modernize this would be to sap the novel of much of its flavour.

ACKNOWLEDGMENTS

Well over twenty years ago, my father Seamus Treacy and I were discussing Wolfe Tone with Tom Flanagan of the University of California at Berkeley, who was doing research for what would become *The Year of the French*. In passing, Tom mentioned that Tone had written a novel. Many years later, when I was beginning to switch my career focus from domestic to academic, that memory came back. With encouragement from my husband Seamus Deane, then Professor of English at University College Dublin, I began to search for the novel, and soon found it in the National Library of Ireland.

I would like now to pay tribute to the Library Staff there for their co-operation in facilitating access to it and to other sources. I am particularly indebted to Dr Kevin Whelan, who has shown continued enthusiasm and support for my project. I would also like to thank Dr Terence Brown of Trinity College, Dublin, who provided early encouragement. I recall too the pleasure of discussing *Belmont Castle* with Marianne Elliott at a time when she was immersed in the life of Tone in preparation for her biography. I also thank Professor John Dillon of Trinity College, who showed sustained interest in this work, and whose generous impulse drew it to the attention of Lilliput Press. To Lilliput, I express gratitude, especially to Brendan Barrington, whose astuteness in questioning the text re-awakened in me the joy of my early research.

Finally, I would like to dedicate this work to my children, Conor, Ciaran, Emer and Cormac, whose love and critical acumen supported me from start to finish.

INTRODUCTION

NOTES

1. See Francis O'Kelly, 'Wolfe Tone's Novel', *Irish Book Lover*, vol. 2 (March–April 1935), p. 47; M.J. McManus, 'When Wolfe Tone Wrote a Novel', *Irish Press* (24 December 1934); 'The Man Who Stole Wolfe Tone's Books', *Irish Press* (1 July 1942); *A Bibliography of Wolfe Tone*, privately printed (Alex. Thom & Co. Ltd, Dublin, 1940); E.R. McClintock Dix, *Catalogues of the Library of E.R. McClintock Dix*, National Library of Ireland, MS 5366; see f.11 for mention of *Belmont Castle*.

2. *The Autobiography of Theobald Wolfe Tone*, ed. Barry O'Brien, 2 vols (Dublin, Cork & Belfast, n.d.), I, p. 16.

3. Quoted in F. O'Kelly, *op. cit.*, p. 47.

4. Tone, *Autobiography*, p. 16.

5. See attributions of letters in chart on page vi, below contents listing.

6. See Francis Hardy, *Memoirs of the Political and Private Life of James Caulfeild, Earl of Charlemont* (London, 1810), p. 424. See also P. Murray, 'Art and Architecture' in *The New Cambridge Modern History*, ed. A. Goodwin, VIII (Cambridge, 1965), pp. 96–115.

7. Sampson, *A Faithful Report of the Trial of Hurdy Gurdy at the Bar of the Court of King's Bench, Westminster 1794* (Belfast, 1794). The witness for the prosecution of Hurdy Gurdy is a French horn which replies to questions by citing the apt titles of popular tunes.

8. Tone, *Autobiography*, II, p. 128.

9. Tone, *Autobiography*, I, p. 27. Patrick Byrne was named by Tone as being implicated in the insurrection by the discovery of papers belonging to Lord Edward Fitzgerald. See *Autobiography*, II, p. 330.

10. Quoted by F. O'Kelly, *Irish Book Lover*, p. 47.

11. Tone, *Autobiography*, I, pp. 27, 212.

12. See *Autobiography*, I, p. 212 (May 1795); 'I sold off all my property of every kind, reserving only my books, of which I had a very good selection of about 600.'

13. *Belmont Castle*, Letter XXI.

14. *The Gentleman's and Citizen's Almanack, Registry and Directory* of 1787 (vol. v, p. 81) names: Stephen Radcliffe, Governor of Schools and Charities; Earl of Charlemont, Governor of the Foundling Hospital (appointed 1772); Sir Lucius O'Brien Bt (Archbishop of Cashel), Governor of the Blue Coat Hospital (appointed December 1781); H. Jebb Kt, physician 'without reward' to Mercer's Hospital, opened August 1734, also Simpson's Hospital in Great Britain Street for 'the poor, decayed, blind and gouty men', incorporated by Act of Parliament in 1780. Cf. Letter XXX. See also *Watson's Almanack* (1784), which lists the Lords Lieutenant and the members of the most honourable Privy Council, including: James, Earl of Charlemont, Kt of St Patrick, Palace Row; Murrough, Earl of Inchiquin, Kt of St Patrick, (Town House), Kildare Street; William Ball, Barrister-at-law, Exchequer Street.

15. The appointment to the Prerogative Court, which had formerly been made by the Crown, was delegated to the Archbishop of Armagh, so that the Ecclesiastical Court and the Prerogative Court were a single body, holding its meetings either in the Judge's own house or in the Chapter Room of St Patrick's Cathedral. As a consequence, there was no secure custody for wills and records. When Radcliffe took over as Judge, he provided a building and transferred original documents to Henrietta Street, where they remained until they were moved to the Public Records Office and then to the National Library of Ireland, where they now reside. See Sir Arthur Vicars, *Index to Prerogative Wills of Ireland, 1536–1810* (Dublin, 1897); Rev. James B. Leslie, MRIA, *Clogher Clergy and Parishes* (Enniskillen, 1929); G.D. Burtchaell &

T.V. Sadleir, *Alumni Dublienses; A Register of the Students, Graduates, Professors and Provosts of Trinity College in the University of Dublin, 1593–1860* (Dublin, 1935), p. 690. We know that John Radcliffe, Judge of the Prerogative Court and Vicar-General of Dublin, was buried in Donnybrook in 1843. See Rev. Beaver H. Blacker, *Brief Sketches of the Parishes of Booterstown and Donnybrook in the County of Dublin* (Dublin, 1784), p. 38, where it is recorded that Radcliffe 'devoted himself with untiring patience to the publick service, combining abilities of the highest order with spotless integrity; to the poor, a sure benefactor'.

16. John Lodge, *The Peerage of Ireland; or A Genealogical History of the Present Nobility of that Kingdom*, 7 vols (Dublin, 1789), II, pp. 44–5, 58–61; III, pp. 152–5 & 177–8; VII, pp. 162–4.
17. Hardy, *Memoirs of Charlemont*, p. 147.
18. *Autobiography and Correspondence of Mrs. Delany*, ed. Lady Llanover, 6 vols (London, 1811), II, p. 416.
19. Hardy, *Memoirs of Charlemont*, p. 184.
20. Charlemont extended hospitality to the Hickman O'Brien relatives at the expense of the Caulfeilds. See Maurice Craig, *The Volunteer Earl* (London, 1948), p. 151.
21. The demesne is well described in *The Volunteer Earl*, pp.122–5, 198–202.
22. Mrs Delany mentions a certain other Miss Blandford who, like our heroine, brings to her marriage a 'jointure' of 'three thousand pounds' (*Autobiography and Correspondence*, I, p. 478).
23. Tone, *Autobiography*, I, p. 16.
24. Edward Synge, *A Letter to the Reverend Stephen Radcliffe, Vicar of Naas* (Dublin, 1725), pp. 2, 6.
25. Charles Forster, *Life of Bishop Jebb D.D.F.R.S., with a selection from his Letters* (London, 1836), p. 23.
26. *Ibid.*, p. 30.
27. Richard Jebb, *A Reply to a Pamphlet entitled, Arguments for and against the Union* (Dublin, 1799), p. 15.
28. *Ibid.*, p. 18.
29. *Ibid.*, p. 44.
30. *Ibid.*, p. 8.
31. *A Letter of Remonstrance*, p. 44.
32. *Ibid.*, p. 14.
33. *Ibid.*, p. 18.
34. *Ibid.*, pp. 24 & 31.
35. *Ibid.*, p. 43. Richard's brother John was equally shocked by the 1798 Rebellion. Trinity College students formed a corps of which, 'till the suppression of the rebellion, Mr. [John] Jebb was an active and influential member'. See Forster, *Life of Bishop Jebb*, p. 34.
36. Inglis, *The Freedom of the Press in Ireland* (London, 1954), pp. 203–4.
37. Thomas Goold, *A Vindication of the Rt. Hon. Edmund Burke's Reflections on the Revolution in France, in answer to all his opponents* (Dublin, 1791), pp. 142–3.
38. William Curran, *Sketches of the Irish Bar*, 2 vols (London, 1855), I, p. 185.
39. *Ibid.*, I, pp. 184–6.
40. *Belmont Castle*, Letter V.
41. *Ibid.*
42. Goold's reasons for leaving France in 1790 were not only connected with the Revolution. His sexual escapades were sufficiently notorious to create the rumour that 'the dogged jealousy of royal husbands' had been stimulated by the suspicion that 'the lazy stream of reputed legitimacy had been quickened by a tributary rill of Munster blood'. Curran, *Sketches of the Irish Bar*, I, p. 187.

43. Thomas Goold, *An Address to the People of Ireland on the Subject of the Projected Union* (Dublin, 1799), pp. 88, 97.
44. *Ibid.*, p. 61.
45. C.J. Smith, *Chronicle of the Law Officers of Ireland*, ed. Henry Butterworth (London, 1839), p. 67, lists: '1816 Richard Jebb Second Serjeant; 1823 Thomas Goold A Justice; 1823 John Ball A Justice'.
46. Goold, *An Address* , pp. 83–4.
47. *Ibid.*, p. 107.
48. Edward Lodge, *Portraits of Illustrious Personages of Great Britain, with biographical and historical memoirs of their lives and actions*, 20 vols (London, 1835), XI, Portrait 6, 'Charles Watson Wentworth, the Marquis of Rockingham', p. 5.
49. *Belmont Castle*, Letter VII.
50. *Belmont Castle*, Letter I.
51. Sir Jonah Barrington, *Personal Sketches of His Own Times*, 2 vols (London, 1827–32), I, p. 33.
52. *Ball Family Records*, p. 156.
53. *Gentleman's and Citizen's Almanack* (Dublin, 1782), p. 2.
54. *Ibid.*
55. *Ball Family Records*, p. 157.
56. See *Art and Oratory: Bicentenary of the College Historical Society, 1770–1970* (Dublin, 1970), Section 5 (published by the National Gallery of Ireland for Trinity College Historical Society). See also William B.S. Taylor, *History of the University of Dublin* (London, 1845), p. 477.
57. The 1804 edition of the *Index* adds as subtitle 'as appear to bind Ireland'.
58. *Index*, Section no. 8, 'Rebellion'.
59. Joshua Edkin (ed.), *A Collection of Poems, most original, by several hands*, 2 vols (Dublin, 1789), II, p. 131.
60. *Ibid.*, 'Epistle from the Author at the Middle Temple to his Friend in Dublin', II, p. 163.
61. Tone, *Autobiography*, p. 16.
62. John Rocque, 'Chorographer to His Majesty', *Survey of City, Harbour, Bay and Environs, with improvements and additions by Mr. Bernard Scale* (Dublin, 1777).
63. The pursuit by Belville of Lady Georgiana Shirley, with the suitor's reiterated lament for his lack of fortune a dominant motif, probably owes a good deal to the gossip surrounding the immense wealth that had passed from Mildred Mary Margaret Ball of the Shirley branch of the Ball family in Dublin to the Balls of Drogheda, c.1788. Charles Ball married Mildred Mary Margaret and, on his death, left large estates and fortune to her sister, Miss Shirley Hamilton. Among the later beneficiaries of this will was a niece who died unmarried at 5 Clare Street, Dublin, in 1873, forty-nine years after William 'Index' Ball died intestate in the same street—whether in the same house or not we do not know. But we do know that, in the period between the death of 'Index' Ball and that of the niece, a solictor named Benjamin Ball had premises at the same address. It is likely that two solicitors, sharing the same name and carrying on their business in the same street, if not necessarily from the same address, were related.
64. Tone wrote the Belville letters to Georgiana Shirley and Jebb wrote the letters from Georgiana to Belville. There were many connections between Jebb and the Ball family. The Ball brothers John and Charles, sons of the Rev. Stearne Ball (1720–77), like Jebb and Goold, wrote pamphlets on the Union. John, the older of the two, was MP for Drogheda (1796–1800) and again like Jebb and Goold, a sergeant-at-law (1806–13). Thus there are lines of connection between Jebb, Goold, the Balls of Drogheda and 'Index' Ball in Dublin. There is even

record of a protracted quarrel in the Ball family, relating to a disputed will of 1785, settled by a ruling made by Jebb in his capacity as Judge in 1825 and finally accepted in 1829. (*Ball Family Records*, p. 156.)

65. *Universal Magazine and Review or Repository of Literature* (Dublin, November 1790); quoted by F. O'Kelly, *Irish Book Lover*, p. 47.

66. *A Short Review of the Recent Affair of Honour Between His Royal Highness the Duke of York and Lieutenant Colonel Lennox, by a Captain of a Company in one of the Guards* (London, 1789), p. 27.

67. *Autobiography and Correspondence*, II, pp. 9–10.

68. *Belmont Castle*, Letter III.

69. *Autobiography and Correspondence*, II, p. 10.

70. *Belmont Castle*, 'The Editor to the Reader', p. 35.

71. Among the plays staged was J. Home's *Douglas* (Belfast, 1766), performed in Kirwan's Theatre, Galway, in 1783. Dick Martin played the villain, Lady Elizabeth Vesey played the heroine opposite Tone. The villain, in killing the innocent young boy, drives the frenzied heroine Matilda (whose name may be echoed here by that of Lady Myrtilla, the lover of Clairville in *Belmont Castle*) to kill herself by jumping over a cliff. This aspect of the play is reflected in the Lord and Lady Middleton/Scudamore affair.

72. *Belmont Castle*, Letter VI.

73. *Ibid.*, Letter XII.

74. Quoted in Shevawn Lynam, *Humanity Dick: A Biography of Richard Martin MP* (London, 1975), p. 60.

75. *Belmont Castle*, Letter XXIX.

76. Lynam, *Humanity Dick*, p. 82.

77. *Ibid.*, p. 80.

78. *Ibid.*, p. 85.

79. *Belmont Castle*, Letter XIX.

80. *Ibid.*, Letter XXIII.

81. *Ibid.*, Letter XVII.

82. *Ibid.*, Letter XII.

83. *Ibid.*, Letter XXIII.

84. *The Fair Penitent* (1703), Otway's *Venice Preserv'd* (1682), and Home's *Douglas* (1766) were not only part of Lady Vesey's theatrical repertoire but are also used in the novel as important points of reference to the whole story of the Vesey affair(s). In the final act of *The Fair Penitent*, in which Lady Vesey had played the leading role as Calista, her father Sciolta consoles her in her dying moments with the thought that posterity might forget her sins: 'Let Silence and Oblivion hide thy name' (V, i). But Tone's references to the play have the effect of parading Lady Vesey's errors, rather than hiding them.

85. Marilyn Butler, *Romantics, Rebels and Reactionaries: English Literature and Its Background 1760–1830* (Oxford, 1981), p. 21.

86. See *Belmont Castle*, Letter XXIV, and *The Sorrows of Young Werther*, 2 vols (Dublin, 1790), II, pp. 100–13 (Letters LXVIII–LXXVI).

87. *The Fair Hibernian*, 2 vols (Dublin, 1789), I, p. 187.

88. *Belmont Castle*, Letter I.

89. *The London Review* (November 1788), p. 348.

90. *Belmont Castle*, Letter I.

KEY TO PRINCIPAL CHARACTERS AND PLACES
Real-life models are given in brackets

THE EARL OF BELMONT [William, 4th Earl of Inchiquin]

LADY GEORGIANA SHIRLEY, daughter of the Earl of Belmont [possibly modelled on a member of the Shirley Ball family]

LORD EDWARD MORTIMER, son of the Earl of Belmont, just returned from a Grand Tour in Italy and France [combines elements of Murrough, 5th Earl of Inchiquin, and Lord Charlemont]

CECILIA, daughter of the Earl of Belmont

SIR JOHN FILLAMAR, father of Lady Clairville [James Caulfeild, Earl of Charlemont]

LADY FILLAMAR, guardian of Juliana Blandford and mother of Lady Clairville

MISS JULIANA BLANDFORD, an orphan of little fortune

LORD CLAIRVILLE [Richard Martin]

LADY ELIZA CLAIRVILLE [Elizabeth Martin, Lady Vesey]

THE HON. CHARLES FITZROY SCUDAMORE, suitor of Lady Clairville [Theobald Wolfe Tone, with elements of Richard Martin and Mr Petrie]

LADY MYRTILLA MIDDLETON, lover of Lord Clairville, former lover of Scudamore [based on stage roles of Lady Vesey]

LIEUTENANT COLONEL HENRY NEVILLE, friend of Scudamore and suitor of Georgiana Shirley [a lieutenant in the Coldstream Guards]

MONTAGUE BELVILLE, suitor of Georgiana Shirley [William 'Index' Ball]

SIR JAMES DASHTON, a young fop of fortune, suitor of Juliana Blandford then of Cecilia [Sir Thomas Goold]

BELMONT CASTLE, home of the Earl of Belmont [Lord Charlemont's house and estate at Marino, Dublin]

GROSVENOR SQUARE, home of Sir John and Lady Fillamar [Charlemont's London home]

ELWOOD FARM, rented home of Belville [Ball estate bordering Charlemont's]

THE MOOR, home of Mrs Cranford, stepmother to Juliana [a piece of land on which the properties of Charlemont at Marino and the Balls at Moorside were contiguous]

BELMONT CASTLE:[1]

OR,

SUFFERING SENSIBILITY[2]

CONTAINING THE GENUINE AND INTERESTING
CORRESPONDENCE OF SEVERAL PERSONS OF FASHION.

"If you have tears, prepare to shed them now."[3]

DUBLIN:
Printed for P. BYRNE, No. 108,
GRAFTON-STREET,[4]
1790.

1. Here, in the National Library of Ireland copy, appears the signature of J. Boyd, a landowner in Letterkenny, Co. Donegal. He was a contemporary of Tone at Trinity College, Dublin. Boyd confiscated this copy of *Belmont Castle* while acting as head of the company of militia that arrested Tone off the French warship *Hoche* in Lough Swilly in 1798.
2. In the same copy, an unidentified bibliographer has here pencilled in the names of the three authors—'By Wolfe Tone, R. Jebb and J. Radcliffe.'
3. *Julius Caesar*, III, ii, l, 173.
4. These premises were next door to the Royal Irish Academy, which met in Navigation House, Grafton Street, from 1788. The Earl of Charlemont and William Ball were among the founder members. See T. O'Raifeartaigh (ed.), *The Royal Irish Academy: A Bicentennial History 1785–1985*. Byrne was a republican. In later years he sympathized with the United Irishmen and was fined for publishing Paine's *Common Sense*.

DEDICATION

To Mrs. Carden[1]

MADAM,

I trembled lest a mode of address so public should meet your disapprobation;—but my vanity at last has got the better of my fears.

I could not resist the temptation of prefixing to this little volume, as a fairy charm against ignorance and ill nature, the name of a Lady so distinguished for beauty, taste and accomplishments, and in whose person nature and education seem to have contended for pre-eminence. Nor will the world suspect me of flattery when I thus express my admiration of the many nameless graces which adorn your mind and form:—they are most eminently conspicuous to all who have the happiness of hearing your conversation, freed from the restraint of crowded circles, and who behold you in the hour of domestic retirement.

You, Madam, are peculiarly interested in the protection of those pages, since you possess a mind glowing with the modest beauties of real sentiment and unaffected sensibility—they are reflected in your countenance.

---

1. This was probably Elizabeth, wife of John Carden, lieutenant in the Royal Artillery. Both he and his son Andrew died in 1789. Andrew had been a contemporary of the authors at Trinity College. His mother, Elizabeth, was a descendant of the family of Moore Disney of Churchtown, Co. Waterford, an Irish branch of the Disneys of Norton Disney in Northamptonshire, among whom John Disney D.D. (1746–1816) had written *The Works of John Jebb M.D.* (1787). See *DNB* and G.D. Burtchaell and T.U. Sadlier (eds), *Alumni Dublinenses* (Dublin, 1935). Alternatively, it may be Elizabeth Bolton, daughter of Theophilus, who married John Carden at the seat of the Rt. Hon. John Monck Mason at Thornhill, near Barry, Co. Tipperary, in October 1789. Thornhill was Radcliffe's mother's ancestral home. See 'Index to Marriages 1771–1812' in *Walker's Hibernian Magazine* (Dublin, 1813), with an appendix by Sir Arthur Vicars, and J. Lodge, *The Peerage of Ireland, or a Genealogical History of the Present Nobility of that Kingdom*, 7 vols, III, p. 176.

Accept then, Madam, of this humble offering—from one who has the honour to subscribe himself,

Your most respectful,
Humble servant,
The EDITOR
Oct. 17, 1790

THE EDITOR[1]

To the reader

LEST the reader should imagine the following tragic events, like those of the common run of novels, the mere ideal production of an heated imagination, the editor thinks it his duty to undeceive him: all the calamitous circumstances so unaffectedly and so mournfully painted in this series of letters, are strictly and uniformly true[2]—of a date recent indeed.[3]—The editor doubts not that the venerable Earl of ———,[4] though concealed under the fictitious title of Belmont, and the long train of heavy misfortunes which attended that truly ancient and noble house, are well known to many of his more fashionable readers.—The editor himself, from his connections[5] with the Belmont family, is but too well acquainted with them; he has sympathized with the good old earl[6] in all his distresses—and were the tears of sensibility inclined to dry up, gratitude would bid them flow.

---

1. John Radcliffe.
2. Events and circumstances in the novel are taken from the lives of friends and acquaintances of the three authors.
3. The scandal on which the central plot is based, involving Lady Vesey, Richard Martin and Mr Petrie, took place in the summer preceding the publication of the novel. See Shevawn Lynam, *Humanity Dick: A Biography of Richard Martin M.P. 1754–1834* (London, 1975), pp. 70–92.
4. Inchiquin. The 4th Earl's four sons died in their father's lifetime, so his nephew, Murrough, succeeded to his title and fortune. See Donogh O'Brien, *The History of the Earls of Inchiquin* (London, 1949).
5. Radcliffe was related by marriage to the O'Briens of Inchiquin. See J. Lodge, *op. cit.*, II, pp. 58–61, 162–5, 176–9.
6. The 4th Earl was familiarly known as the 'good old Earl'. See *The History of the Earls of Inchiquin*, p. 72.

The simplicity of stile and diction, as well as the soft touching sensibility displayed in the following pages, the editor hopes will plead his excuse in thus agitating so forcibly the public feelings by laying before them a tale of woe so interesting and so affecting.

LETTER I

From Miss Juliana Blandford to Lady Georgiana Shirley

GROSVENOR SQUARE[1]

2 o'clock

NO, my amiable Georgiana, the dissipation of this great metropolis has not weakened the ardency of my affection:—with a calm delight—with a soothing melancholy do I reflect on those happy hours we spent together at Belmont Castle.—The parting sighs of my tenderly lamenting friend still echo in my ears;—still do I behold her beauteous cheeks suffused in tears. Good heavens! what were my feelings on hearing (or rather feeling, for grief denied it utterance) thy last adieu! Amiable sensibility! it pervades every member of the family. The good old Earl sympathized with his beloved Georgiana —Lady Bridget's severity relaxed into pity— and the tears of the venerable domestics bespoke their love for their mistress and the tenderness of their minds.

After a journey rendered in some measure supportable by the maternal assiduity of Lady Fillamar and the penetrating remarks of Sir John[2] upon the country we passed through, we arrived in Grosvenor Square on Monday evening. The intervening time has been employed in the necessary arrangements previous to our public appearance; and till this evening we have been at home.— Sir John's house is spacious; the furniture (chiefly of Lady Fillamar's selection) unites richness and delicacy in a most extraordinary degree. The arrangement of the whole is such as the taste of the possessors would promise; and the entire establishment is formed on a scale of prudent magnificence.

---

1. The London address of James, Earl of Charlemont, was 39 Grosvenor Place.
2. This is the fictitious name assigned to Charlemont.

In my apartment, which has been honoured by the peculiar attention of Lady F., my taste has been most scrupulously adhered to. The anti-chamber is hung with a delicate lilac silk, fringed with silver, elegantly festooned; the chairs to match the hangings; the bed-chamber is hung in the same manner, only with a deeper fringe; and in an alcove is placed the bed, which is formed of the richest chintz, lined with a pale rose-coloured silk, bordered with silver chenille; opposite the bed is my dressing room, from whence I command a view of the distant hills and the intervening country, with all its variety of spruce[3] villas, humble cottages, rich woods, smooth lawns, lofty towers and glittering spires. Here her Ladyship's taste and magnificence have chiefly displayed themselves; the hangings, which like those of the other rooms are of a blue ground, are ornamented with silver flowers, and the chairs are also worked in silver in the richest taste. The furniture of the dressing-table is of silver and of the choicest porcelain. But, what my Georgiana will believe chiefly claims my attention and demands my gratitude, is a book-case stored with a collection of our choicest English authors; here, when fatigued with the impertinence of the drawing room, can I retire and enjoy my favourite Shenstone;[4] charming writer! poet of nature! how often, my Georgiana, have we sympathized with our favourite! how often, when seated in the hermitage, have we lamented the cruelty of Laura![5] The reflection draws fresh tears from thy friend, and this paper will bear to thee the marks of her weakness.

Friday morning, 8 o'clock
The agitation of my mind, from the recollection of our parting scene and of our never to be sufficiently prized delight at Belmont Castle, rendered me unfit last night to give my Georgiana a narrative of the occurences of yesterday, the first day we have seen company.

---

3. Dapper. Etymologically, it means 'brought from Prussia'.
4. There was a Dublin edition of Shenstone, *Shenstone: The Works in Prose and Verse*, printed by Faulkener, 1777.
5. The name of the maidservant in Goethe's *The Sorrows of the Young Werther*. There was a Dublin edition of this novel in two volumes, 1780–1.

Lady Fillamar having announced her arrival to her friends, we had last night a numerous party. Her Ladyship most particularly introduced me to her intimate acquaintance, and by the most endearing solicitude endeavoured to banish that timidity on which the lively Lady Cecilia has so often rallied me. But, notwithstanding her efforts, the consciousness of my own situation and the embarrassment of the rustic, I am afraid, broke forth; but from the kind attention of her Ladyship, the endeavours of some of her guests were employed to overcome my fears. Four or five card tables being formed, the rest of the company, whose characters I shall endeavour to delineate, composed a group where the ordinary topics of dress, fashion, and amusement were discussed with the skill of connoisseurs. Except your Juliana, the only female of this set was a Miss Langville, the only daughter of a Colonel Langville, who seemed to possess many of those qualities which belong to her father's profession. Her person is certainly a fine one, above the middle size, of a commanding air, a countenance strongly marked, an aquiline nose, dark penetrating eyes, and her voice adapted to her language, bold, vehement and decisive. Luckily for your Juliana, she seemed at first sight to conceive an attachment to me; or else her supercilious and awful brow would have encreased my confusion.

Among the gentlemen the most remarkable were a Mr. Belville[6] and a Major Welton. The former, who is the younger branch of an antient family, is about two years returned from the university. To a good person he unites an elegant, though melancholy, languor of countenance, which bespeaks a heart of the tenderest susceptibility; whilst his eyes, enlightened by a peculiar fire, give an irresistible force to his animated conversation. The patrimony of the younger branch being insufficient for his support, he has determined on the profession of the law, and the faint recital I am going to give you of a conversation in which he bore a principal part will convince you that he possesses the most persuasive

---

6. Based on William 'Index' Ball (see Introduction), author of *Index to the Statutes at Large, Passed in the Parliaments Held in Ireland* (Dublin, 1799).

eloquence and the most shining rhetoric. But, first, let me intro-
duce Major Welton to your acquaintance; he appears to be about
forty, of a plain but pleasing countenance, and remarkable for
speaking his sentiments with the most undisguised freedom.

"Sir," said Miss Langville, addressing herself to the Major, "have
you read *The Orphan of the Castle*⁷ yet? I am told it is a charming
novel." "No Madam," replied the Major, "nor do I mean it; I have
no patience with those monstrous relations of improbable virtues,
those absurd caricatures of modern levities, those demi-gods in
laced coats, and goddesses in satin. If we are to have *fiction*, the
bold falsehoods of an Eastern tale are surely preferable; the
author there attempts not to impose on our credulity, he fairly
tells us that we are launching into the ocean of chimeras, and the
phantoms which he raises are but its natural productions: a novelist would blindfold our judgment whilst he inflames our imagi-
nations, and would persuade us that England is really peopled
with such personages as never had any existence but in his own
heated brain." "I am sorry, Sir," said Mr. Belville, "to differ from a
person of Major Welton's acknowledged judgment; but I must say
that our modern novels appear to me in a different point of view,
as a most elegant and refined amusement, and as a delineation, by
no means too flattering, of those virtues and accomplishments of
which the present day, and perhaps the present company (looking
with indescribable expression at his female auditors), could give
the brightest specimens." "And, do you really think", interrupted
the Major, "that there exists at this day a Clarissa, or that the
minutest search could furnish us with a Sir Charles?"⁸ "Do I?"
exclaimed Belville, "may I perish, but I most firmly believe it, most
firmly believe that the present age could furnish us with innumer-
able patterns of female excellence, not inferior to that all-perfect
character"; then sinking on one knee, with an ardor of enthusiasm

---

7. *Emmeline: The Orphan and the Castle* (London, 1788), by Charlotte Smith. Dublin edition in 2
   vols (1789), printed by White, Byrne, Wogan, Moore, Jones and Halpin. Byrne was the publisher of *Belmont Castle*.
8. The central characters in Samuel Richardson's famous novels *Clarissa* (1747–8) and *Sir Charles
   Grandison* (1753–4).

which affrighted and astonished me, he said, "Hear me, high heaven! Tutelary guardian of aspiring virtue, hear the prayer of thy votary! Inspire me to emulate the virtues of a Grandison, as I believe in the exalted perfection of a Clarissa, and may such angelic worth be the bright reward of my zeal in *thy* service, as I entertain the glorious hope of one day meeting with a female equal to the heroine of the pathetic Richardson."

The wild enthusiasm which flashed in his eyes as he spoke filled me with a terror I cannot describe. I trembled all over—and my confusion would have been evident, had not Miss Langville kindly assisted me with her Eau de Luce.[9]

Adieu!
JULIANA

---

9. Luce—a fruit sprung from the rose and luce.

LETTER II

From Lord Mortimer[1] to John Evelyn, Esq.
BRUSSELS

AFTER an absence of three years from my country and my friends, your feelings will tell you what must be mine on the idea of returning. For I trust you will believe that however an extended intercourse with the world may have enlarged my views, and diminished national prejudices, it has not weakened my attachment to my native soil. No, my friend, my Evelyn! my heart beats with fervency for England's welfare; the incomparable pre-eminence of her government and manners have been more fully displayed by comparison with other countries. The honest, bold simplicity of her yeomen, those bulwarks of her strength, the unpolished plainness of her traders, the undaunted eloquence of her senators, and not least, the unsophisticated charms of her daughters, are peculiar to herself; and with double lustre must they appear to him who has penetration to discover and sense to despise the brilliant, but deceitful, tinsel of French manners, and the still more disgusting depravity of Italian morals.[2] Don't, however, imagine that I have travelled with the cankering spleen of the misanthropist; notwithstanding my partiality, I have still remarked and done justice to the soothing urbanity of the one country, and the refined taste of the other; and during my residence abroad, which you know, according to the judicious advice of Lord Chesterfield,[3] has

---

1. The character of Mortimer is an idealized, generic portrait of an heir to an illustrious tradition epitomized by the Earls of Charlemont and Inchiquin.
2. Current sentiments of the period, notably expressed in Francis Hardy, *The Memoirs of Lord Charlemont* (1810), p. 52.
3. Philip Dormer Stanhope, 4th Earl of Chesterfield, *Letters to his Son* (1774).

been chiefly in the capitals of France and Italy, I have met with many characters whose solid worth and brilliant talents would have been an ornament to any country.

The hopes you so fondly entertained, I am afraid, will not for some years be realized. Tho' I detest a life of useless ease, yet the bustle of politics, and the virulence of party, are ill suited to your Mortimer's disposition. It is not, therefore, my design to endeavour at obtaining a seat in the senate; when an event indeed which I hope will be many years distant, shall give me an hereditary voice in the supreme council of the nation, it will be my duty to devote some portion of my time to the interest of my country and to support in some degree the exalted character of my house. The Earls of Belmont have for ages been distinguished as the assertors both of their sovereign's and of the people's rights: and the present age, I trust, will not be witness to their degeneracy.[4] My illustrious father has been careful to instill into me those elevated principles of which his own life has been so noble an example. The princely fortune I shall inherit, the example of my ancestors, the kind partiality of my friends, all, all will urge me on to fame.[5] But till the event I have mentioned shall take place, it is my design to shun the tumult of politics, and to devote myself to the use and enjoyment of my friends, and to the further cultivation of my mind.

I am already preparing for my departure, and in about a fortnight you may expect to embrace

Your most devoted
MORTIMER

---

4. William, the 4th Earl of Inchiquin, was Lord of the Bedchamber to Frederick, Prince of Wales, 1744. He became an MP in 1722 and Governor of Co. Clare in 1741. *The History of the Earls of Inchiquin*, pp. 40–1.
5. Murrough inherited title and large estates for a number of reasons: his four cousins died tragically; the next in line, the father of Sir Lucius O'Brien, was overlooked because of his exorbitant gambling; and Murrough married his first cousin, Lady Mary O'Brien. See *The History of the Earls of Inchiquin*, pp. 83–6.

LETTER III

From the Hon. Charles Fitzroy Scudamore to Lieut. Colonel Neville

HARLEY PLACE

OH! Harry, such an adventure!—"Grace is in all her steps—heaven in her eye"[1]— "Very likely", methinks I hear you exclaim, "but in whose steps? and whose are these heavenly eyes?" Ask not, oh! ask not! Can there be in nature such another?—No, by heaven!

> "When the devout religion of mine eye
> Maintains such falsehood, then turn tears to fires,
> AND BURN THE HERETIC.
> Oh! she is more than painting can express,
> Or youthful poets fancy, when they love."[2]

Cheeks that shame the rose, lips of coral-dye; pearls of orient for teeth; her neck a pillar of alabaster; her chestnut tresses floating in wanton profusion to the gale; her eyes, oh! Harry, her eyes of soft celestial blue, beaming forth bright emanations of tenderness and love; but, her smiles! how shall I describe them? hast thou yet discovered her? or must I add the name? Dull clod! hear then, nor wonder longer at the transports of thy friend, thy doating, captive friend—hear with reverential awe the name of the bright divinity[3] at whose shrine I bow—art thou prepared? Hear in one word, the name of—Lady Clairville,[4] and wonder at my madness if thou canst.

---

1. *Paradise Lost*, I, viii, 488.
2. *Romeo and Juliet*, I, ii, 93.
3. Cf. 'adored her as a deity'; note on Lady Vesey in Tone's autobiography. Quoted in Lynam, *Humanity Dick*, p. 47.
4. Lady Elizabeth Vesey, wife of Richard Martin and erstwhile love interest of Tone. Her fictional name is derived from Clareville, the Martins' house at Clare (now Oughterard), Co. Galway.

Yes, Harry, she it is who has wrought this mighty revolution in the sentiments of thy friend, the once gay and giddy Scudamore;—alas! those days are over; and now, instead of liberty free as air, instead of power despotic over the sex, behold me the humble, sighing slave of this dear, haughty beauty. Yet why do I call her haughty? To me she is affability itself: as yet, however, nothing more than affable—and shall that suffice? No, forbid it honor; forbid it love; forbid it the long roll of conquests to which, or my art fails me, her Ladyship's name must be subjoined—*tout doucement* tho'! No hasty measures to alarm the dragon that with incessant vigilance guards the golden fruit.[5] At present I am her *friend*—do you mark that, Colonel?—*friendship* with woman, you know.—"But in the name of heaven," thou wilt say, "whence comes this sudden attachment?—Where did you meet?—When?—How?—" I will tell thee all.

By the death of my uncle, Harley, you know, I was suddenly recalled from the continent, and by urgent affairs obliged to come down here and enter on the lands and lordships which the good-natured prejudice of the worthy old fellow thought proper to bestow on me. For the first six weeks sinking under the weight of an additional £16,000 per year, fatigued to death with deeds and mortgages, and employed, even till my hand was tired, in signing leases and releases, I could scarce venture out. At length, when I had reduced my affairs into some tolerable order, I one morning mounted my horse, and rode forth in quest of adventure, with a spirit not perhaps exactly coincident with that of the knight-errant of old. In plain English, trusty William had discovered that my steward had a daughter, whom he was pleased to represent as not totally unworthy of the honor of becoming my sultana[6] for the present; and I was determined to call as if accidentally and judge for

---

5. This is Richard Martin, MP and landlord. There is also a probable reference here to the 'Burlesque Operatical Dramatick Farce', *The Dragon of Wantley* (music by John Frederick Lampe, libretto by Henry Carey), which was very popular in Dublin from its first performance in 1738. The hero, Moore of Moorehall, is a dragon-killer as well as lady-killer. See T.J. Walsh, *Opera in Dublin 1705–1797; The Social Scene* (Dublin, 1973), pp. 57–8, 70–2.
6. Wife or concubine of a sultan.

myself; but fortune had better things in store for me. As I was crossing a common which lies between Lord Clairville's estate and mine, I beheld a lady approach on horseback, with whose figure, even at a distance, I was struck; never had I beheld any mortal being yet, so graceful. Whilst I was engaged in contemplating her beauties, the sudden discharge of a fowling piece startled her horse, who darted off like lightning, regardless of his angelic burthen.

In the very direction he pursued—but I am interrupted—"Well, William!"—

"My Lady Clairville is below, sir, in her chariot, and wishes to see you."

I fly to attend her.—In my next you shall hear more.

—Till then—

Adieu!
C.F. SCUDAMORE

LETTER IV

From Lady Fillamar to the Countess of B.
GROSVENOR SQUARE

THE account that I can give you, my dear madam, of Miss Blandford, is very imperfect. But as you express so warm an interest in
the happiness of that amiable girl, I shall give you every information in my power. You are well acquainted with the strict friendship
that subsisted between me and Mrs. Cranford,[1] that exemplary
woman, whose virtues were an ornament to our species, and who
for the last fifteen years had the sole care of my Juliana. How this
office devolved upon her, or the minuter particulars respecting the
birth and descent of Juliana, I know but imperfectly. The mother
of Juliana, who was distantly related to Mrs. Cranford, at an early
age married Mr. Blandford, the son of a merchant, who was
descended from an honourable family. The match being unequal
to the pretensions of Miss Lester (Juliana's mother), was formed
contrary to the opinion of her friends, and all intercourse between
them was cut off. Some losses in business and other misfortunes
obliged Mr. Blandford to undertake a voyage to India; his Lady res-
olutely, and fatally, insisted on accompanying him. The catastrophe was dreadful, the ship was lost and every soul perished. The ill
health and tender years of Juliana, who was then but three years
old,[2] made it necessary to leave her behind. The cruel neglect of

---

1. Note that Mrs Cranford becomes Mrs Crawford some lines later. A Mrs *Crawford* had the leading role in the theatre on the night of the infamous mêlée between Richard Martin and Lord
George Fitzgerald in 1783. See *Humanity Dick*, p. 48. Martin reports: 'Mrs Crawford, I found
had been engaged to play for a few nights in Crow St. Theatre and I determined to see her
Belvidera.' This is the name of the heroine in Otway's *Venice Preserv'd*. See also Sir Jonah
Barrington, *Personal Sketches of his own Times*, 2 vols (London, 1827–32), II, p. 268.
2. When Francis Caulfeild, brother of James, Earl of Charlemont, drowned in a shipwreck in the
river Liffey near the port of Dublin, his three-year-old daughter was with him in the boat. See
Introduction, p. 9.

her nearer relations called upon the humanity of Mrs. Cranford; she adopted the amiable orphan, and in her conduct displayed a love truly maternal. Of the rest it is needless to say anything to your Ladyship. You are acquainted with the recent death of my ever to be lamented friend. On the first news of her illness, Sir John and I flew to the Moor,[3] and arrived just in time to receive her dying adieu. In words hardly intelligible, she conjured me to fulfil the part of a mother to her Juliana, and assured of my compliance, she resigned her soul in peace. To alleviate Juliana's loss, and fulfil the injunctions of my friend, I consider myself bound by every tie of friendship, and the pious office is rendered more sacred by the uncommon virtues of my ward. Such amiable sensibility, such purity of mind, such ardency of affection, such effusions of gratitude, we may look for but seldom can find. The graces of her person, angelic as they truly are, are the least part of her merit. With such accomplishments, it might appear too worldly to lament her want of fortune. Mrs. Crawford's chief income, your ladyship knows, was a jointure, and the expanded benevolence of her soul did not permit her to amass wealth. Three thousand pounds was all she could bequeath her Juliana; but selfish as the world may be, such exalted excellence can never have cause to lament the absence of wealth.

After Mrs. C.'s decease, Lord Belmont, who you know lived within a few miles of the Moor, and of whose veneration for the worth of my friend I need not inform you, invited us to spend some time at Belmont Castle. The kindest assiduities of the Earl, and of his amiable daughters, were employed to alleviate the distress of their friend. The attachment which had long subsisted between them was cemented by this event, and their efforts were not quite unsuccessful in dissipating her grief, tho' still the remembrance of her beloved guardian visibly affects her spirits. The entertainments of the metropolis we judge might be useful, and we accordingly have given up our intention of spending the winter at the Forest,[4] and are settled for some months in Grosvenor Square.

---

3. The Moor, as marked on the Rocque map of 1777, is a stretch of land on which the properties of Lord Charlemont at Marino and of the Ball family at Moorside adjoin one another.

4. Also marked on the Rocque map, as part of the Ball property.

I need make no apology to your Ladyship for the length of this letter; nor is it I hope necessary to assure your Ladyship with what truth I am

Your most sincere friend,
and devoted servant,
C. FILLAMAR

LETTER V

From Miss Juliana Blandford to Lady Georgiana Shirley
GROSVENOR SQUARE

WHY, my Georgiana, did I leave the peaceful mansion of Belmont Castle? Why did I refuse thy kind entreaties?—Hear the cause of my complaints and judge of their justice. Last night I accompanied Lady Fillamar to a ball given by Sir James Dashton.[1] Sir James is about five and twenty, with a fortune of seven thousand pounds a year, a shewy person, an uncommon proficient in dress and the other fashionable accomplishments, and not a little vain of his merits. The company was extremely numerous and splendid, the decorations of the rooms to the last degree rich and singular, and the dress of the entertainer characteristic of his disposition. His hair was turned before in small irregular curls, it flowed loosely behind from a bunch of pink ribbon, to an immoderate length, and the strong aromatic scents that issued from it could alone tell you that powder had been employed. His coat was of a pale rose-coloured sattin, lined with the most delicate blue; the cape and cuffs like the lining, richly embroidered with silver; his waistcoat white tissue, trimmed with sable, his shoes of black sattin with red heels, and tied with bunches of pink ribbon intermixed with silver

---

1. Sir Thomas Goold. This is one of the most authentic portraits of a known individual in the novel; see Introduction. On Goold see also William H. Curran, 'Serjeant Goold' in *Sketches of the Irish Bar*, 2 vols (London, 1855), I, pp. 183–93. Goold was a friend and disciple of Burke, whose view of the French Revolution he defended in *A Vindication of the Right Hon. Edmund Burke's Reflections* (Dublin, 1791). He also gained attention for his anti-Union pamphlet, *An Address to the People of Ireland* (Dublin, 1799). For an account of this see R.B. McDowell, *Irish Public Opinion 1750–1800* (London, 1944), pp. 159, 164–5, 250–2. His address to the final protest meeting (against the Union) of the Irish Bar in 1799 is recorded in *A Report on the Debate of the Irish Bar, Sunday the 9th December, on the Subject of an Union of the two Legislatures of Great Britain and Ireland* (Dublin, 1800). This is noticed by Oliver MacDonagh, *States of Mind: A Study of Anglo-Irish Conflict 1780–1980* (London, 1983, 1985), p. 15.

foil. So extraordinary a figure you may suppose raised the surprise of the Company; their complaisance for their entertainer could not overcome their propensity to laughter; and to any eyes but those of Sir James, blinded by vanity, it was evident that he was the object of their mirth.

What was my astonishment to behold him approach and address me in the following words! "The divine Juliana cannot be ignorant of the cause of this entertainment—will she crown the night by granting me the honor of her hand? Will she give fresh triumph to my already established taste?—and will she exhibit a perfect example of the most accomplished pair of dancers that England can display?"

Amazed by the singularity of this address, I was at a loss for a reply. "Sir," said I, "the honor"—but Sir James cut me short, by respectfully and with an air of triumph seizing me by the hand, while as he was leading me up the room, Lady Fillamar, who is intimate with him, stopped us. "Sir James," said she, "you cannot be serious? Consider the etiquette of the assembly—consider the affront you offer to the married Ladies—the Duchess of C. in particular—do, Sir James; let me entreat you to hear me." 'Twas all in vain. "By heaven!" he exclaimed, in a tone that startled the whole room, "Majesty herself should not gain that pre-eminence which I give to Juliana. No, bright nymph," throwing himself on one knee, "I here swear by the irresistible divinity of love to devote myself to thy service, to assert thy superiority over all thy sex, and to give to thee the triumph of conquering, and holding in adamantine chains, the proud stubborn heart of the hitherto victorious Dashton. Let the hapless nymphs that I have captivated lament my cruelty;[2] let the kind fair ones who have yielded to me complain of my perfidy; to thee I sacrifice them all: and by all the Gods, by the sacred Majesty"—here surprise, terror and confusion overcoming me, for the room was in a tumult, and the whole company in astonishment was gathering around, I fainted away. In this situation I remained for some time, but the kindest assiduity of Lady F. and some of the company recovered me. While I was in this situation,

---

2. See Introduction, note 42.

Sir James, I am informed, was almost frantic; he emptied his entire bottle of *eau de luce* in my face; then, for he is most uncommonly active, leaped over the heads of the intervening crowd, and with frantic rage, roaring to his domestics, dispatched them all for physicians and surgeons; by the time however he returned I was recovered, and had prevailed on the kind Lady Fillamar to let me go home. Sir James insisted on accompanying us, but Lady F., representing the delicacy of my situation and the impropriety of his leaving his company, prevailed on him to desist; but what was our surprise on arriving at Grosvenor Square to find Sir James there before us, breathless, bespattered with dirt, and drenched with rain! for impatient and too thoughtless to order a carriage, he ran or rather flew before us, regardless of the frantic oddness of his dress, of the length of the way, the dirt of the streets, or the wetness of the evening. Here, before we could recover from our astonishment at his appearance, he poured out a thousand apologies for the distress he occasioned—and was proceeding in the same impassioned strain when Lady F., fearful of a relapse, conjured him to leave me; that on another opportunity he might declare his intentions; and that his presence was absolutely necessary to dissipate the confusion which so extraordinary a proceeding must have occasioned. With difficulty he was prevailed upon to depart, not without vowing that he would to-morrow make me a tender of his person and fortune.

And now, my Georgiana, will not thy sympathetic bosom join in lamenting my cruel destiny, when I tell you I can never love the enamoured Sir James? And, good heavens! what may be the consequence of a refusal to a man of his impetuous temper and extraordinary vanity? That he is rich, handsome, young, accomplished,[3] I cannot deny; but is there not an incontroulable destiny, is there not a mighty power which governs the affairs of love? His fortune, his rank, are beyond my expectations, but can fortune—can rank confer true happiness? No, there is "nought but love can answer love, and render bliss secure".[4] The amiable Lady F. is a convert to

---

3. Similar to the description of Dashton given in William Curran, *Sketches of the Irish Bar*, I, p. 185.
4. Unidentified.

this opinion; the unhappy disagreements between her daughter and Lord Clairville, though there is every external requisite on each side, convince her that it is from the union of hearts alone that conjugal bliss can spring; and I doubt not I shall have the approbation of my kind protectors in rejecting the offer of Sir James.

Oh! my Georgiana, how do I wish I were once more at Belmont Castle, to pour into thy faithful bosom the griefs of thy afflicted

JULIANA

LETTER VI

From the Hon. C.F. Scudamore to Colonel Neville
HARLEY PLACE

AS well I recollect, for the violence of my passion bids defiance to connexion, I ended my last, my dear colonel, with an account of the imminent danger of Lady Clairville, from the fright of her horse;—in the very direction he pursued, a precipice occurred, down which, if not instantly stopped, he must have dashed himself and the loveliest of women.—What was to be done?—The urgency of the occasion precluded deliberation, so I at once darted the spurs into Nero, who, as if inspired with the spirit of his master, flew over every impediment.—In an instant I had overtaken and seized the reins of her steed, not a dozen yards from the edge of the yawning gulph, and dismounting, caught her in my arms scarce half alive—the colour forsook her cheeks, darkness sealed her swimming eyes, and her countenance was enwrapped in the pale livery of death. I despatched her servant, who was by this time come up, to a neighbouring cottage for some water, and mean while applied my *Eau de luce*; my cares were soon crowned with success, and I saw, with transport saw, her bright eyes resume their lustre, the colour revisit her cheeks, soon indeed heightened to a crimson glow, on finding herself in the arms of a young fellow whose looks, I am afraid, very intelligibly spoke his emotions.—In short, I found at once that I had redeemed her life at the expence of my liberty, and in an instant joined the sighing train who in happier days have so often been the ridicule of Neville and his Scudamore.

As soon as she was recovered sufficiently to speak, she thanked me for the assistance I had been so happy as to afford her, and told me in a manner sufficiently intelligible that Lord Clairville, if he were to have the honor of seeing me at the Grove,[1] would add his thanks to hers—that was as much as to inform me that she was married—*tant mieux*! I know Lord Clairville; I know him to be a scoundrel; I know that in one instance he has supplanted me—

> "For which, when I forget it, may the shame
> I mean to blast his name with, stick on mine!"[2]

Sweet, sweet revenge! if I be not even with him, wife for mistress, but no matter; all this is mystery to you, colonel; hear it then explained—and from my narrative see what a thing the mind of man is.—A short time before I set out to the continent I was introduced to the widow of *le feu chevalier Middleton*, a woman whose character, if drawn at all, must be by negatives; she is *not* old; she is *not* ugly; she is *not* ignorant; she is *not* deformed, nor totally unaccomplished; with a great deal of vivacity and an intemperance of passion restrained, if restrained, only by the fear of losing at once the remnant of character still remaining to her, she thinks mankind born for her pleasures, and with this idea are all her connexions formed. As her constitution prompts her to an indiscriminate passion for our sex, so does a most intemperate vanity insinuate to her that this ardency is reciprocal; and to such extravagantly ridiculous lengths does this silly passion carry her, that I am satisfied she never held a conversation with a man five minutes, without a thorough conviction of his ambitiously aspiring to that honor which, sooth to say, like many others has at present lost its original value by an indiscriminate distribution.—How I could be so mad or blind to notice such a compound is utterly inexplicable, but so it was—in short, her Ladyship was kind, I was successful, and was willing to persuade myself I was happy.

Just at this moment it was my uncle Harley's pleasure I should pass a few months on the continent. I parted from Lady Middleton with a concern for which I now despise myself—a concern which

---

1. This feature is also marked on the Rocque map of 1777.
2. Lothario to Rossano in Nicholas Rowe, *The Fair Penitent*, I, i.

she had the art to persuade my inexperience was mutual; and she retired to her seat in Berkshire, with vows of eternal constancy, and that her life should be that of a recluse till my return.—Well, sir—My Lord Clairville, whose demesne adjoined her Ladyship's, soon introduced himself, and with little trouble took quiet possession of all my honors; and, as I have since learned from the maid of this wanton, the light credulity of Scudamore was the constant theme of their discourse.—And shall I with impunity be held up the scoff of the loose hours of Clairville and his paramour?—Shall the wrongs of the divine Lady Clairville go unrevenged as well as mine?—No!—by all the mingled powers of Love and Jealousy, by all the stings of mortification I have already felt, by all the glowing transports I hope soon to feel in the arms of that angelic woman, I will be revenged and tell the proud peer to his beard, "Thus diddest thou!"[3]

Thus, then, I stand at present. I have got *les entrées libres* at the Grove; his Lordship is much at Lady Middleton's, who is, as I told you, most conveniently contiguous; Lady Clairville is, with every other feminine perfection, the first performer[4] on the *pianoforte*[5] I have ever heard.—You know I am not contemptible on the German-flute;[6] I have in consequence the honor to accompany her. She sings too:—

> "Such melting strains as would create a soul,
> under the ribs of death!"—[7]

---

3. *Hamlet*, IV, vii, 58.

4. In 1787, when the Martins played in John Home's *Douglas* (1756) to most of the Galway nobility and gentry at Kirwan's theatre, the *Freeman's Journal* critic stated that Lady Vesey was exceptional for 'the justness of her elocution, the marked propriety of her emphasis [and] the uncommon grace of her attitude'. Tone had fallen in love with her during extended rehearsals for this play, in which he too had a part. He considered her the best actress he had ever seen. See *Humanity Dick*, pp. 46–7, 67.

5. *piano e forte*; invented in Padua in 1710, it became increasingly popular, especially in Vienna, in the later eighteenth century.

6. Cf. note 9, p. 91. See also F.J. Crowest (ed.), *The Story of the Flute* (London & New York, 1914), p. 43.

7. Milton, *Comus*. A masque of *Comus*, with music by Thomas Arne, was first performed at the Aungier Street Theatre in Dublin in 1741. It remained popular for the rest of the century. See T.J. Walsh, *Opera in Dublin*, pp. 59–60.

And the divine canzonets of Jackson[8] afford me a happy opportunity of at once gratifying my passion for music and silently advancing my suit with her Ladyship.

Already I can see her moved; but I must be cautious—she shall not know her danger till it is too late to avoid it.—She must, she shall be mine—then, ye mighty gods, what a treasure!—But I must fly to meet her!—Yes, adored Eliza, to thee do I return with an ardor surpassing that of the travelled turtle[9] to his mate—with rapture do I haste to contemplate the mild radiance of thy celestial eyes; to hear thy accents sweeter than the mellifluous strains of plaintive Philomel, and touch thy snowy hand, to whose soft seizure the cygnet's down is harsh.—

Adieu, my friend,
Believe me ever yours,
C.F. SCUDAMORE

8. William Jackson, organist at Exeter Cathedral from 1777, wrote sacred music, sonatas and ballad operas. The most famous of the latter was *The Lord of the Manor*, first performed in Dublin in 1781 at the Crow Street Theatre. The libretto was written by General John Burgoyne, the man who lost the battle of Saratoga in the American War of Independence. See T.J. Walsh, *Opera in Dublin*, p. 200.
9. 'No turtle for her wandering mate shall mourn.' Epilogue to Rowe's *The Fair Penitent*, in which Lady Vesey played a leading role.

LETTER VII

From Sir James Dashton to Colonel Watworth[1]
GUILDFORD LODGE

BAFFLED!—despised!—rejected!—and by whom, ye mighty Gods!—by a flirt—a child of fortune—curse on her beauty!—yes, her *beauty*, for still must I allow her charms.—By the great G—Watworth! yes, and may the furies tear my distracted heart.—I rave!—I rave!—what will the world say?—every charm called forth, never was drest to such advantage!—Lamont[2] had exerted all his art, and never did'st thou see such a coat.—St. Pierre[3] too, had given me[4] such curls—oh! Watworth—but by the high heavens I'll be revenged—give my fortune to an hospital,[5] cut off my hair, and turn Monk[6]—but then the world!—and all my ambitious schemes;—no, my country shall have the advantage of my disap-

---

1. A conflation of the name Watson Wentworth (see Introduction. p.14). See E. Lodge, *Portraits of Illustrious Personages of Great Britain, with biographical and historical memoirs of their lives and actions*, 20 vols (London, 1835), IX, 'The Marquis of Rockingham', p. 4ff. He was highly recommended by Lord Charlemont for his 'integrity of mind as founded in the best school of Whiggism'. Hardy, *Memoirs of Lord Charlemont*, p. 109.
2. Perhaps based on Lambart, a clothier and perfumier of Brabazon Row. See Watson's *Gentleman's and Citizen's Almanack, Registry and Directory* (Dublin, 1784–5).
3. A French hairdresser or *frizeur*.
4. At this point in the NLI copy an unknown hand has written 'Portrait of T. G—d by R J–bb'.
5. Jebb's uncle, Sir Richard Jebb, and Radcliffe's grandfather, Stephen, together with Sir Lucius O'Brien, uncle of Murrough and close friend of Charlemont, gave voluntary help to a number of newly established Dublin hospitals in 1787, including Bluecoat, Mercer's and Simpson's. The *Gentleman's and Citizen's Almanack* records this.
6. At the opening of the Pantheon in London in 1772, Lord Charlemont and friends arrived disguised as monks. Mrs Delany records: 'The quadrille of the new order of Monks that appeared at the maskerade is the subject of conversation ... I have enclosed you an account of the Pantheon maskerade with all the explanation of the maskers' names that I can get. Sir Chas. and Lady Bingham, Lord Charlemont and Sir Thomas Tancred were the quadrille.' (*Autobiography and Correspondence*, I (Series 2), p. 417.)

pointment.—The army, the army is the line—there will I display myself—my merit and fortune and connexions must raise me—'tis the line of glory.—But then, my political consequence, my seat in parliament—no, Watworth, wait till the next session, and if I don't annoy Pitt[7]—I am no boaster, but you know my fame at Oxford, and by the mighty Gods it shall not be tarnished—no—curse me if it shall.

But of this girl—you heard of my intended ball—you heard of the expectations formed—all blasted. Some cursed, untoward, womanish crotchet seized her brain, and as I was leading her up the room she fainted. Fillamar insisted on carrying her home— and enamoured as I was, I determined to accompany her—there being no room in the carriage, and my brain quite distracted, I forgot where I was—I forgot that there were fifty other carriages at the door—and I did not perceive the cataract of rain that descended on my bare head—but, regardless of everything, from Portland Place did I set out as running for a wager, and arrived in such a pickle as might well excite the merriment of graver women than Lady F.—and Juliana.—The powder and pomatum rendered fluid by the rain had descended down my face in thick streams, the dirt of the streets had totally obscured the original colour of my dress, and nothing was visible but one continued mass of mud.

To heighten my confusion, the rascally servants laughed aloud at my appearance, and when I left the house (which I soon did at Lady F.'s intreaty) the whole fraternity, cooks, chambermaids and cullions, were collected in the hall to enjoy my grotesque figure.—Home did I return, and, forgetting my company and exerating the whole world, I went to bed and locked myself up from the intrusion of my intimates, who were coming in crowds to be

---

. Dashton/Goold, infamous for his boasting, is here imagining himself in the role of Watworth/Wentworth. Because of Wentworth's vanity and inexperience, he was the butt of the opposition in parliament. Pitt claimed that his only contribution lay in his 'creditable name'. However, Lord Charlemont's admiration for him was almost unlimited. In the year of his death in 1782, Wentworth wrote to Charlemont, declaring that he would 'continue to act towards Ireland and towards promoting the common good of the Empire with the same zeal and liberal ideas'. He believed that national and private friendship go 'hand in hand'. (Hardy, Memoirs of Charlemont, p. 231.)

satisfied of the cause of the confusion and to have a subject of scandal to embellish for the next day.

Of the rest of the night I know nothing but from report—the company, astonished at the disappearance of the entertainer, soon retired, and by this time I suppose the ballad singers are composing ditties, and the print-sellers preparing to stick me in their windows.

I have already seen paragraphs in the newspapers, informing the public "with infinite concern, that it is feared Sir James Dashton's intellects are injured"—already telling who is to have the guardianship of my fortune, and giving, in proper newspaper form, an account of my ancestors, estates, titles, &c.

Unable to bear this I instantly flew down here—but I will be revenged.—The proud Juliana (for I am informed she means to reject my offers, but if she has an opportunity, curse me) shall be mortified—she shall be a witness of my splendor.—I am determined to have the greys, I don't care for the price, I will give the 1000 guineas and Hatchet shall make me such a phaeton!—but enough, Tom, it is needless to say more—you know the indignant spirit of—

Thine ever
JAMES DASHTON

P.S. Are you to be at Elwood races?[8] I am invited to spend the time at Belmont Castle, to meet Lord Mortimer who is hourly expected

---

8. Both Goold and Wentworth had an abiding interest in horses (see Introduction).

LETTER VIII

From Montague Belville, Esq., to John Evelyn, Esq.
ELWOOD FARM

YOUR friendly bosom, my dear Jack, must doubtless be alarmed
at my sudden departure from the metropolis; but your alarm will
cease when you are told that Lady Georgiana Shirley is the beautiful magnet that has drawn your friend so far from town, and
Evelyn—you cannot[1] sure have forgot the impression she made
on my heart last winter, at the opera, on the night of Storace's[2]
benefit; how she diverted my attention from *Mozon*[3] and how '*Chi
mi mostra*' and the charming duet of '*Piche cornacchie*'[4] escaped my
usual *encore*. All that night her charming idea incessantly presented itself to my enraptured fancy and deprived me of rest. I strove
to compose myself, but in vain;—tossed by a tempest of love, I
now rose on the anchor of hope, now sunk on the billows of
despair:—a momentary calm succeeded, but it was only to make
the returning storm more terrible.—At last the orient sun
appeared in the chambers of the east; I arose—dressed myself—
swallowed my chocolate in a hurry; and ran about nine to

. An unidentified hand has written in the margin of the NLI copy at this point in the text, 'Portrait
of J.W. B—l by T.W. Tone'.

. Ann Selina Storace (1766–1817), an English soprano of Italian descent, was an excellent
actress and a universally popular singer. After spending some time in Venice and Vienna, she
returned to a successful career in England in 1788. She was sister to the celebrated compos-
er Stephen Storace. See J. Ashton, *Old Times: A Picture of Social Life at the End of the
Eighteenth Century* (London, 1885), p. 204. The operas of Stephen Storace, particularly *The
Haunted Tower* and *No Song no Supper*, had a vogue in Dublin in the late 1780s. See T.J.
Walsh, *Opera in Dublin*, pp. 278ff.

. Thomas Mozon, an Englishman of French extraction who acted in the Dublin
theatres c.1744. Among his songs and essays was *The Kilruddery Hunt* (London, 1762). His
wife, née Edwards, was a well-known singer on the Dublin stage.

. Arias from the opera *Schiavi per amore*.

Portland Place, In hopes of gaining a sight of my adored Georgiana.—But, oh! Evelyn! to my inexpressible grief, the Shirley family had set out a few hours before in their coach and six for Belmont Castle!

In all the frenzy of a despairing lover, I walked with disordered steps to my lodgings in Wimpole Street; where, as my dear Evelyn may remember, I found a letter informing me of the illness of my uncle, Lord Belmour, at Naples, and of his wish I should attend him there.—My surprise at this unexpected summons, as well as my haste to obey it, prevented me from acquainting you with the secret of my passion for the too lovely Georgiana.—

When I arrived at Naples I found my uncle Lord B. had recovered, so as to be in a condition of compleating the tour of Italy.[5]— I accompanied him—and thus the summer passed away without my being able to procure an interview with the Idol of my soul.[6]— But why do I thus teize my Evelyn by the recital of circumstances with which he is already acquainted? I know not, unless it is that to a lover passionate as I am, to repeat and dwell on the particulars of his misfortunes be painful pleasure and a soothing melancholy.—To be brief, I last Friday found that a farm near Belmont Castle[7] was unoccupied; and conceiving that with such an opportunity I might probably make an impression on my Georgiana's heart, or at least enjoy the superlative blessing of living near her, I immediately hired post horses, and now rent the farm of the good old Earl—my success has been greater than my most sanguine hopes could have presaged.—I have seen my Georgiana! the loveliest, tenderest, fairest of her sex!—at Church I was so lucky as to arrest her attention.—I gazed on her with unutterable rapture—her eyes met mine—and oh! happy presage—oh! omen most lucky—the dear angel blushed "cælestial rosy red",[8] and he

5. See Introduction for William Ball's opinion of the Grand Tour. On the Grand Tour, see Peter Murray, 'Art and Architecture', in A. Goodwin (ed.), The New Cambridge Modern History, vol. viii (Cambridge, 1965, repr. 1979), pp. 96–101.
6. Horatio to Callista in Rowe's The Fair Penitent, II, i: 'Idol of thy soul!'
7. The Ball family to this day owns farmland bordering on Charlemont's original estate at Marino.
8. William Shenstone, 'Comparison'—'her cheek's celestial red'—in The Poetical Works of William Shenstone, ed. G. Gilfillan (Edinburgh, 1854), p. 143.

enchanting bosom heaved with soft emotion.—How changeable, my Evelyn, are the affairs of men!—the weather itself is not more liable to fluctuation!—I who three days since was the unfortunate, am now the happy Belville;—three—yes, Evelyn, three days have raised your friend from the lowest abyss of despair to the highest pinnacle of joy and happiness.—In my next I shall give you a description of this delightful and romantic farm.—Adieu!—congratulate your friend on his rapid success in his passion—and let me add too in his farming—for, believe me, Evelyn, since I arrived here on Saturday morning, I can say with my favourite, the sublime Shenstone, that

> "I seldom have met with a loss,
> Such health do my fountains bestow;
> My fountains all bordered with moss,
> Where the hare-bells and violets grow."[9]

I have just learned from Laura, Lady Georgiana's favourite woman, that the Earl had proposed, as a lover to my charmer, Col. Neville; but that she had yesterday expressed a violent disapprobation of his addresses, and this morning gave him an absolute refusal.—Laura too informs me that Lady Georgiana is particular in her enquiries about me, and that she often mentions her deliverer in terms of the warmest approbation.—Adieu—I am extacy itself—but yet I feel a terror I cannot account for and which damps my happiness—what may not the temper of the slighted Neville forbode my Georgiana!—but I'll not think on it. If she once is mine—where is the arm so strong can tear her from Belville?—United to my Georgiana, no fear but that of offending her shall disturb my quiet—the malice of disappointed villainy I'll defy.

---

9. From Shenstone's most famous poem, 'A Pastoral Ballad'; part of the first stanza of Part II, 'Hope'. *Poetical Works*, p. 151.

Adieu! assure yourself of the unaltered friendship of

Yours
MONTAGUE BELVILLE

LETTER IX

From Colonel Neville to the Hon. C.F. Scudamore
BELMONT CASTLE

I give you joy, my dear Scudamore, with all my heart, of your success with her Ladyship—don't be discouraged at any repulse she gives you—did she not tell you she owed her life to you; then why not compound the debt with her honor?—You have set me on fire by your description; and a little cruel piece of prudery has inflamed me *in propria persona*; so that, damn me if I am not between two fires, as we say in the Coldstream.[1]—Do you recollect Lady Georgiana Shirley, daughter of the Earl of Belmont?—If you have ever once seen her you *must*;—the dear, delicious angel; the very essence of Virtue, yet, the very figure of Temptation, with a fair complexion, dark hazel eyes, nut-brown hair, a neck like alabaster, and a heart like *ice*, egad—for, damn me if ever I could melt it—"and if Colonel Neville could *not*," I hear my Scudamore exclaim, "what mortal can?"—Aye, but one Belville has—a fellow with the cant of virtue and *all that*—but I'll have revenge.—I broke my passion to Lady Georgiana, told her I doated on her, sighed, fell at her feet, and acted an hundred extravagancies—her answer was, she hated me.—What shall I do to be revenged?—Counsel me, my dear fellow, tell me how I shall triumph over the chastity of my Georgiana, and the pride of Belville.

Adieu,
Yours ever,
HENRY NEVILLE

---

1. The Coldstream Regiment owes its origin to General Monck, appointed by Cromwell after the Irish campaigns to invade Scotland. See R. McKinnon, *The Services of the Coldstream Guard* (London, 1921), pp. 1, 496.

LETTER X

From Miss Juliana Blandford to Lady Georgiana Shirley
GROSVENOR SQUARE

Friday, 12 o'clock

OH, my Georgiana! how would'st thou have been torn between hope and fear, hadst thou been a witness to the situation of thy friends—but I forbear the excruciating thought. The idea of my Georgiana's feelings distracts me more than the recollection, horrid as it must be, of my own danger.—Already do I see the sympathetic tear bursting from thy eye, already does thy breast throb at perusing so alarming an introduction; but it is cruel to keep you in suspence, and distracted as my thoughts are, I will endeavour to give you a circumstantial account of the proceedings of last night.

I accompanied Lady Fillamar to the play. Mrs. Siddons[1] appeared in the character of Isabella, and the house, you may suppose, was uncommonly crowded. The late extraordinary accident at Sir James Dashton's brought on me the eyes of numbers, and among the rest, of one whom I could perceive stealing the most eager glances; he appeared to be about one and twenty, but such a mein! such a figure! OH, my Georgiana, they beggared all description, but difficult as may be the task, I shall attempt to pourtray him.

His person was one of the most commanding, and, at the same

---

1. Sarah Siddons (1755–1831), the greatest tragic actress of the period. She was particularly famous as Lady Macbeth, as Belvidera in Otway's *Venice Preserv'd* and as the heroine in Rowe's plays *The Fair Penitent* (1703) and *Jane Shore* (1714). So great was her popularity in Ireland that Murrough, 5th Earl of Inchiquin, built a tower in honour of her at Rostellan Castle Co. Cork, in 1777. (This was before she achieved her great fame in London in 1782. See Mark Bence-Jones, *Burke's Guide to Country Houses* [London, 1978], p. 214.) Elizabeth Martin, Lady Vesey, played the part of Calista in amateur productions of *The Fair Penitent*. See J. Ashton, *Old Times*, p. 58.

time, the most graceful, I ever beheld; the most happy union of strength and elegance reigned throughout.—The Apollo of Belvedere[2] itself must yield to him as a model of excellence.

His complexion, though not delicately fair, was as beautiful as the most happy composition of the brightest vermillion and the most brilliant pearl.—But his eyes! his eyes darted such looks as penetrated to the very soul, at the same time that there shone from them such a god-like benignity as inspired confidence and love.

The first glance that I directed to him I felt my face suffused with a burning blush, and I had such sensations as I never before experienced. I was embarrassed to such a degree that all the woes of the divine Siddons could not chain down my attention, and in vain did I attempt to prevent my eyes from wandering to that fascinating object.—The charming stranger certainly perceived my situation, for often as I dared to steal a glance I perceived his eyes rivetted; and then when he found himself discovered, he endeavoured to conceal his emotions by directing his attention to the play, though his distracted look, and sudden blush, easily told where his thoughts were employed.

In the middle of the fourth act, we were surprised by the cry of fire.—All was in the most alarming confusion—my eyes were, by I know not what impulse, directed to the stranger; and I perceived him struggling through the crowd, and his looks directed towards me. Several gentlemen, coming to our assistance, urged us to entrust ourselves to their care, and I saw no more of the charming unknown.

Through the dreadful tumult I was torn from Lady Fillamar, when overcome by terror, heat, and fatigue, I fainted away.—In this situation I must have continued a considerable time, for on my recovering I found myself in a strange room with several females and a gentleman, none of whose faces I knew, busily employed to recover me.—I instantly exclaimed, "Where am I?—

---

2. The most famous of the Roman statues at this period, selected for special praise by Winckelmann in *Reflections on the Painting and Sculpture of the Greeks*, translated by Fuseli in 1765.

where is Lady Fillamar?—tell me, tell me, is she safe!"—"Don't be alarmed, my angel," cried the man or rather monster,[3] as he afterwards proved;—"Lady Fillamar is safe, and there are none here but friends.—Be not alarmed, my angel!"—then beckoning to the females, they left the room.—"Blest be this propitious night," he cried, "that gives me possession of such an angel!" and instantly the wretch attempted to seize me in his arms;[4] but springing from him, in an agony of despair, I shrieked aloud for help. "Save yourself that trouble," exclaimed the monster, "all here are privy to my design.—You had better therefore yield with a good grace to that which you must undergo"; and again was he seizing me in his arms: I fell at his feet, and conjured him by every sacred name to spare a hapless maiden, when in the very instant, the door burst open, and who should appear but the very stranger whose regards I had attracted at the play-house.—"Oh my guardian angel!" I exclaimed, "Save me, save me!" and I ran into his arms.—"Be assured of my protection," replied the heavenly stranger, "be assured of thy safety. And thou, vile monster," said he, with a voice like thunder, "thou who couldst dare to violate such distrest innocence, instantly begone, or dread the effects of that resentment which thy brutality may well inspire."— "Begone!" exclaimed the wretch—"No! not till I have secured my prize, and chastised thee for so insolent an intrusion."—With those words he sprung towards me—but the gallant stranger, presenting himself before me, saved me from his unhallowed touch.—They instantly engaged, for they were both armed, and in a moment the hated monster fell.—The stranger then, calling to the vile inhabitants of the house, ordered them to take care of their abominable guest.—Then supporting me down the stairs, for the terror I had

---

3. There is a particular contemporary reference possible here. In the years 1788–90, a number of women in London were attacked and stabbed by a man known as the Monster. See J. Ashton, *Old Times*, pp. 247, 254–6.

4. Forced abduction of women was a marked feature of Irish life in the latter part of the eighteenth century. Sometimes love was the stimulus; more often it was the desire to possess the woman's fortune. See Mrs Delany, *Autobiography and Correspondence*, I (First Series), p. 108; Louis M. Cullen, *The Emergence of Modern Ireland 1600–1900* (London, 1981), pp. 245–8; Frances A. Gerard, *Some Fair Hibernians* (London, 1897).

undergone rendered me almost unable to walk, he handed me into a coach, and by my desire ordered him to drive to Grosvenor Square.

Before I had time to offer my acknowledgments, he addressed me in these words: "How happy do I esteem myself that the commencement of an acquaintance with the most lovely of her sex should give me any claim on her friendship; how supremely happy that I should be the means of rescuing from ruin such divine excellence."—"Oh, sir," I exclaimed, "how shall I thank you! Where shall I find words to express the grateful overflowings of my soul?—But what an opinion must you have formed of me from such a situation as you discovered me in; or by what providential chance were your steps directed to that vile house?"—"Be composed, fair excellence," he replied, "tomorrow will unravel all— suffice it to say, for the present, that after making eager search for you through all the avenues of the theatre, some chance, surely more than human, directed me through the street where I discovered you; as I passed by a house some female shrieks assailed my ear, and the feelings of a man urged me to learn the cause— with a drawn sword I rushed through a crowd of wretched women who endeavoured to oppose my passage, and at length gained the apartment where you were confined—but we are already arrived. Tomorrow, with your kind permission, I shall wait on you, when I shall hope to find you recovered from the alarms of this disastrous night."—The carriage stopped, and having conducted me up the steps, the stranger disappeared.

I found Sir John and Lady Fillamar in a state little remote from distraction at my absence; and their joy at my recovery was little removed from insanity. But when I related to them my miraculous escape, we all fell on our knees and joined in thanksgiving to that beneficent Being by whose divine Providence I had been rescued from destruction.—But I am called away—Oh my Georgiana!

Adieu!—how I burn with impatience! and yet, how I tremble to approach him!

* * *

JULIANA BLANDFORD, in continuation—
Three o'clock

Oh!—my Georgiana!—would'st thou believe it!—the lovely stranger is thy brother—'twas he—'twas—'twas Lord Mortimer rescued thy Juliana—'twas he saved her from destruction!

When I came down to the drawing-room, Lady Fillamar arose, and taking me by the hand, "My Lord," said she, "allow me to present to you Miss Blandford—my Juliana, this, your deliverer, is Lord Mortimer, the brother of your Georgiana."—Luckily I had reached a chair, for my tottering limbs were no longer able to support me—a deadly paleness and deeper crimson alternately had possession of my face; I attempted to articulate, but my voice refused its office. Your noble brother perceived my confusion, but he kindly devised an excuse, and attributed it to the effects of last night!—"Miss Blandford, I perceive, is still too much affected by the confusion of the playhouse."—Amiable delicacy! He carefully avoided to mention that part of the night in which he had so large a share.—"My Lord," I cried, "how shall I thank"—"No thanks, I insist upon it—let not the too sensible Juliana encrease her agitation by mentioning so disagreeable a subject. The character of Miss Blandford", continued he, "has long since been well known to me. I had imagined it flattered beyond what human nature would admit, but now I see that even the warm partiality of such a friend as Georgiana could not do it justice."—But I am denied time, my Georgiana, to relate to you the particulars of this interesting conversation. Lord Mortimer informed us that, impatient after three years absence to embrace a father and his sisters, he proposed to set out for Belmont Castle in the evening, and he now waits for this letter.

How, my Georgiana, how do I envy your feelings; how do I anticipate your joy on the reception of such a brother! But, unwilling to detain him, I must bid you a hasty adieu.

JULIANA

LETTER XI

From Lady Georgiana Shirley to Miss Juliana Blandford
BELMONT CASTLE

IT is true, my dearest Juliana, I am in possession of all the generality of females call blessings: title, youth, affluence, and, if I may give any credit to my glass, some little share of beauty; yet, still your Georgiana is not happy;—a too expressive sensibility renders her the weathercock of every nice, every delicate, every tender feeling. Good Heavens!—I tremble at the thought of meeting a too amiable youth!—into what strange perplexities and misfortunes might not my too sensible heart transport me!—into what sorrows too might not *hers* lead my Juliana!—I tremble for *you*—I tremble for *myself*; for, my dear, my amiable friend, are not our souls of the same temper?—has not Providence given to Georgiana and Juliana the same tender sympathies, the same delicacy of feeling, the same elegance of sentiment? But my Papa has sent for me—adieu—for the present!

* * *

"You sent for me, Papa?"—"Yes, my child, my love, my Georgiana!—You know I have ever consulted your happiness, ever watched over your education with a father's tenderness." "Ever, my dear Papa, you ever have"—cried I, melting into tears;—"you have ever been my tenderest, best Papa; you have been too, too indulgent, and your Georgiana will never be forgetful of your kindness." "I did not send for you, my child, to upbraid you; but to acquaint you with my efforts for your welfare.—You are now seventeen, and it would give me the truest pleasure to see you settled, before the grave levels my honors and titles with the dust:—I have, therefore, my child, provided you with a husband—one who"—I

heard no more—at the name of *husband,* my sight failed me—a
cold tremor shook my knees, and I fell senseless on the floor.—I
lay in this state of insensibility six hours. When I recovered, I
found myself in bed—my father, my brother, my sister Cecilia, and
my faithful Laura, weeping around me.—They tell me I am at
times delirious—and that then I can repeat nothing but—*husband*—and *Juliana.* I am now pretty well recovered—the embraces
of a beloved brother have wrought in me the happiest of changes;
Laura too consoles me; the poor creature sheds with me tear for
tear—but my naughty brother interrupts me.

"Well, sister, my sweetest Georgiana, you look charmingly this
morning—what, writing?—and to our lovely friend Juliana"—and
he sighed.—"Why do you sigh, brother?"—"Have I not cause?" he
said—and laid his hand upon his heart—"OH, too enchanting
Juliana!" and he burst into tears.—Your Georgiana could not
refrain from mingling her tears with his—he begged me to intercede for him with my lovely friend—melted as I then was how
could I refuse?—He kissed my hand with rapture—called me his
angel, his amiable, amiable sister—expressions how flattering
from a brother so beloved, so doated on as Mortimer by his
Georgiana!—"Must I bribe my Georgiana's intercession?"—and
he held me out your letter which he almost devoured with kisses.

* * *

In continuation.
How have you alarmed me, my dear, my amiable friend!—what a
strange variety of emotions did your last raise in my soul.—Joy, sorrow, anger, surprise, terror, despair, hope and anxiety, each in turn
agitated your Georgiana, and reigned triumphant in her sympathetic bosom. "What", cried I in tears, "must have been the feelings of my Juliana, at finding herself at such an hour, and in such
a house, in the arms of such a monster!—Gracious Heaven!—
What must have been the terrors and wild despair of Lady Fillamar
at the loss of her lovely charge?—All-seeing Providence, how art
thou entitled to our most heart-felt acknowledgments for my
Juliana's miraculous escape!—What sincere joy do I feel at her

deliverance!—What joy too that Mortimer, the brother of her friend, her Georgiana, was the happy instrument of her release; he loves, doats on my Juliana—she too is not insensible to his perfections! Happy, happy Georgiana!—could she to the name of friend add the more tender and endearing appelation of—*sister*. Mortimer, my brother, the amiable Mortimer, has confessed to me the secret of his heart; he sighs for Juliana—do my lovely friend, pity your Mortimer; pity the brother of your Georgiana!—Assuage his sufferings—else let me sweetly blame my Juliana.—Cecilia too, the lively Cecilia, joins in my intreaties; she vows she will ever love her dear, sweet, little Juliana—adieu—pity Mortimer—pity your Georgiana—*husband*! I tremble at the name!——

GEORGIANA SHIRLEY

LETTER XII

From the Hon. C.F. Scudamore to Colonel Neville
HARLEY PLACE

SINCE my last, oh, magnanimous Colonel, I have been within a point of ruining myself for ever.—All my bright prospects, all my glowing hopes, had my imprudent haste nearly destroyed. My cursed impatience!—oh, I could rave—but soft!—these transports better suit another place, and other ears than thine.—Thank heaven, the danger is past and has left, yes, my friend, it has left this golden consolation, this extatically transporting reflection behind it, that she, my fair one, my Eliza, does not—angels catch the sounds, and waft them through the bright air on your purple pinions—does not hate the happy Scudamore; prepare for an inundation of joy, and bliss unutterable.

Yesterday evening I walked over to the Grove—the setting sun gilded the western hemisphere with a rich Tyrian dye, the fleecy flocks and feathered songsters[1] had retired to rest—all save the love-lorn Philomel, who in plaintive strains re-echoes thro' the grove.[2] My heart was softened—all nature seemed in union with my feelings.—"Give me my Eliza, heaven," I cried, "or end at once this worthless being!" Such were my reflections on turning into the house, where—oh, transport unutterable! oh, bliss unspeakable!— I found that urgent business had drawn Lord Clairville to London, whence he was not to return for three days—to my designs three ages.[3]—I approached the music-room, and heard the organ

---

1. The words are taken from a canzonet by Jackson. See *The British Musical Miscellany*, vol. I (London, 1734).
2. Passage in the style of Shenstone.
3. Tone claimed that Richard Martin neglected his wife by frequent absences which allowed him, Tone, to declare his suit. See *Humanity Dick*, p. 47.

breathe forth such dulcet symphonies as might well proceed from the fingers of a divinity.—Happy *Pergolesi!*[4] never before were thy conceptions realized.—I stole in softly—the *adagio* she was playing entered into my soul—the lovely Eliza too seemed to feel it, and at the close reclined her head pensively on her snowy hand.—She heaved a balmy sigh, so languishly sweet that my soul was wrapped in Elysium. *My* bosom too heaved responsive—she heard me, turned suddenly her lovely head, and with a blush that made the ruby pale, exclaimed, "Good Heaven, Mr. Scudamore!" "Be not alarmed, Madam," cried I, "nor with the poisoned drop of your indignation dash the cup of felicity which the beneficent hand of Fortune offers to my lips.—Nay, start not, stir not, fly not, loveliest of women!—I adore you, worship you—my waking thoughts, my sleeping ideas are occupied with your beauteous image.—Oh, happy sleep! in whose bounteous arms I find a refuge from my torture, for then is my Eliza kind—but, alas, whither has my passion hurried me?—I thought in eternal silence[5] to have buried that carking, corroding care which consumes my vitals, wastes my strength, and leaves me but the shadow of what once was Scudamore!"—and I burst into tears.—Her lovely hand still remaining clasped in mine, I pressed it in an agony of distress to my eyes and my forehead.— "Rise, Sir", exclaimed the dear angel, with a firm dignity of manner which petrified my soul and numbed all my mental and corporal faculties like the stroke of a spent thunderbolt, "rise, Sir; I have already heard too much—more than friendship can demand or honour warrant—tyrant honour! cruel love! oh my torn heart! rise I beseech, command you—consider if we should be seen." "Seen my life, my angel," I exclaimed, "who is to see?

---

4. Giovanni Battisti Pergolesi (1710–36), one of the earliest composers of *opera buffa*. His *La Serva Padrona*, first performed at Naples in 1733, is his comic masterpiece and was influential in displacing the heavier and ornate grand opera. Pergolesi's music is regarded as a characteristic response to the cry of 'Back to nature!'. *La Serva Padrona* and Rousseau's *Le Devin du Village* were jointly produced in Paris in 1752. See W.S. Pratt, *New Encyclopedia of Music and Musicians* (London, 1924). *La Serva Padrona* was performed in Dublin in 1762 and 1764. See T.J. Walsh, *Opera in Dublin*, pp. 332–3.

5. Given the notoriety the affair would gain from this revelation of it, Tone is obviously mocking Lady Vesey, her husband and himself.

———Come thick night
And pall thee in the dunnest smoke of hell;
Nor heaven peep thro the curtain of the dark
To view my happiness."[6]

Oh, my Lady Clairville!—Gods, thank you!"—and I caught her in my arms—but, ah, my friend, what is this world? Vain are our hopes of sublunary bliss;—even at the very moment when man, presumptuous, short-sighted man, delights himself with a bright perspective of ideal happiness, the storm arises, the clouds condense, and the whole airy vision is dashed by some left-handed God!—Pardon this observation, my dearest friend, it flows spontaneous from my heart, and I cannot—I wish not to restrain its feelings.

The dear, terrified angel, shocked at my audacity, instantly disengaged herself from my embrace, and throwing herself at my feet, her lovely hair dishevelled, her bright eyes suffused in tears— "Kill me, barbarian," she exclaimed, "draw thy bright sword, sacred ever to honour and to justice, and sheathe it at once in this bosom while it is yet spotless,[7] nor sully the purity of her who to you and for you would sacrifice her life, her soul, her all except her honour!"—Curse on my weakness—wouldst thou believe it, that I, thy Scudamore, should from my dearest purpose be baffled by sighs and prayers and woman's lamentations?—Yet, oh, my Neville, hadst thou beheld as I did the lovely mourner prostrate on the carpet—at your feet—had you heard her piercing cries— had you felt her briny tears, more bright than orient pearl, fast dropping on your heart—had you, I say, felt all this, what had been your feelings?—You must, yes, my friend, must as I did have passed the glorious, golden opportunity—I know his generous

---

6. Scudamore's version of *Macbeth*, I, v, 48–52:
        'Come, thick night,
        And pall thee in the dunnest smoke of Hell,
        That my keen knife see not the wound it makes,
        Nor Heaven peep through the blanket of the dark
        To cry, 'Hold, hold!''
7. See Introduction, pp. 21–2, for comment on this passage.

nature, ever tremblingly alive to the soft suggestions of philanthropic humanity, must at once have sunk before the united force
of agonizing beauty, innocence in distress, and purity more bright
than the purity of the angelic choir.

Adieu, my friend!—the monitory clock on the great stairs, with
iron tongue and mouth of brass,[8] warns me to rest—one—two—
all nature is at peace except thy Scudamore, within whose breast
an ague of tyrannic love despotic reigns—now firing my soul with
glowing hopes—now freezing it with chilling fears—alas!—oh, for
an eternal sleep!—Morpheus now lays his leaden mace upon my
eyelids—once more adieu!—I go to dream of my beloved—dear,
enchanting charmer!—but I must to bed!—to bed! to bed!——

C.F. SCUDAMORE

---

8. Shakespeare, *King John*, III, iii, 38:
> 'The midnight bell
> Did, with his iron tongue and brazen mouth,
> Sound on.'

LETTER XIII

From Lady Georgiana Shirley
to Miss Juliana Blandford
BELMONT CASTLE

OH, my dearest Juliana, how am I plagued to death with Colonel Neville's odious assiduities; for this, my friend, is the husband my Papa would have provided for me. My Juliana knows my papa's violent attachment to noble birth and antiquity of family. Colonel Neville is, it seems, next heir to a dukedom, and descended from the great Earl of Warwick, so famous in the plays of Shakespeare. Vain honours! Empty sounds! Give me the man I love and a cottage, and I'll resign, with pleasure, luxury and nobility of birth to the ambitious and the insensible.—I will try, my dear, to give you a description of Col. Neville—he is tall and well made, with a good complexion, white teeth, and the air of a man of fashion—but his eyes—oh, Juliana!—his eyes are impudence itself—none of that bashful timidity, that respectful expression, is conspicuous in them, which distinguishes the virtuous lover—his eyes convince me he is a rake—think of it my friend, he dared to look stedfastly at your Georgiana; and with a smile too—presumptuous man! His conversation too is not chaste, for he dares in my presence to laugh at sensibility.—When he addresses me, his voice, 'tis true, assumes a softness; but ah! my Juliana, I can discover in it none of those amiable hesitations, those faultering accents, periods interrupted by sighs and blushes, and those starts of passion so sweet, so amiable in love—which Werter uses to his Charlotte—poor unhappy Charlotte—amiable—but an unfortunate Werter!—how oft has the recital of your pure but luckless passion drawn the tear of sympathetic tenderness from mine eye!—My tears blind me—why hast thou, Oh Governor of the universe! given me a heart so soft—so susceptible of tender impressions?

I blush my dear to tell you that a young farmer, who has within these few days become a tenant of my papa's, has raised in my breast an emotion which neither the Marquis of Beaujolais nor Col. Neville have ever been able to inspire me with. Oh, heavens, my unhappy lot!—that my heart should feel for a person, to an union with whom it is impossible my papa should ever consent!—Oh, my Juliana, must I confess to you my weakness?—I adore him.—"How did my Georgiana meet this victor," mayest thou say, "Where?—when?—how?"—You shall hear— at church I perceived his eyes constantly directed to our seat;—his countenance open and touching to an extreme, arrested my attention.—I ventured to steal a look at this too amiable youth, his eyes met mine;—we were both confused, and cast our eyes downward. He blushed, and your Georgiana underwent a total suffusion; his eyes spoke unutterable things, and I thought I could perceive a silent tear steal gently down his cheek.—"Perhaps," cried I to myself, "perhaps he doats on some more beautiful, more happy maiden —for her that tear flows; for her that sigh is heaved. Lady Georgiana, he does not aspire to thee—collect thyself—let not a rustic see thy weakness.—How would the Earl of Belmont," thought I again, "think of his daughter, his Georgiana, if he supposed her capable of bestowing a thought on a peasant— a cottager?—He would cast out your poor, forlorn Georgiana from his bosom, as a stain upon his blood."—Adieu—I go to make enquiry about this charming stranger.—Perhaps he may not be what he seems; perhaps, but let me not indulge the flattering delusion. Adieu! a thousand times adieu.—Pray for your

GEORGIANA SHIRLEY

LETTER XIV

From Montague Belville, Esq., to John Evelyn, Esq.
ELWOOD FARM

WHEN I gave my friend a promise of describing to him the beauties and situation of my farm, I was not aware of the arduous task I had undertaken; however, as my enemies could never upbraid me with breaking my word, I should consider myself void of every principle of honor and gratitude did I prove less faithful to my friends.

    This delightful and romantic spot, to which, since my arrival, I have given the name of Elwood Farm, is beautifully situated on the slope of a hill, enamelled with daisies, violets and purple heath. Close to the door of my humble cottage runs a meandering rivulet, which serves at once for beauty and for use—when the fatigue of my spirits has thrown a pleasing languor over my limbs, the murmuring of this limpid stream "invites one to sleep"[1]—and when the golden sun darts on it its chearing beam, the reflection of this glassy rivulet casts a silver brightness over the windows of my rural dwelling.—[2]

> "Oh! Sun, how pleasing are thy rays,
> Reflected from the polish'd face
> Of yon refulgent streams."——[3]

And, Oh!

---

1. Shenstone, 'A Pastoral Ballad' (1743), *Poetical Works*, p. 121.
2. This is adapted from Shenstone's miniaturized landscape garden at the Leasowes, Halesowen. He called it a *ferme ornee*. His *Essays on Men and Manners* contain his views on 'landskip' gardening. Richard Graves (1715–1804) gives a description of it in his *Recollections of William Shenstone* (1788), and wrote a novel, *Columella*, based on Shenstone's life.
3. From Shenstone's 'An Irregular Ode, After Sickness. 1749', in *The Works in Verse and Prose*, p. 139. The first line should read: 'O Sun! how pleasing were thy rays.'

"Ye streams, if e'er your banks I lov'd,
If e'er your native sounds improved,
May each soft murmur soothe my fair,
Or Oh!—'twill deepen my dispair."[4]

A little beyond the rivulet, my friend, lies a small but beautiful and level lawn, where my fleecy flocks brouze in safety, and where my tender lambs and lambkins sport and ba-a in lovely native innocence.—And for my cattle—Oh! Evelyn,

"Not my fields, in the prime of the year,
More charms than my cattle unfold."[5]

The feathered songsters,[6] too, ope their little throats, and it is impossible to conceive—

"From the plains, from the woodlands and groves,
What strains of wild melody flow;
How the nightingales warble their loves
From thickets of roses that blow."[7]

And would my Georgiana but once deign to visit my humble cottage, I have had so many rehearsals of my little natural musicians—

"That when her bright form shall appear,
The birds shall harmoniously join
In a concert so soft, and so clear,
As—she may not be fond to resign."[8]

But, alas! my friend, all these *natural* beauties, I fear, will decay through your Belville's inattention—the rivulet no longer purl; the feathered songsters warble; nor any fences restrain my cattle, for, since—

---

4. Shenstone, 'Song XVI', from *Poetical Works*, p. 181.
5. Shenstone, 'A Pastoral Ballad', *Poetical Works*, p. 151
6. Tone repeats the phrase from Jackson, perhaps as a comment on Ball's uninspired mentality.
7. 'A Pastoral Ballad', *Poetical Works*, p. 152.
8. *Ibid.* These lines follow on directly from those preceding. The first word should be And, not That.

"Georgiana vouchsafed me a look,
I never once DREAM'D of my vine—
May I lose both my pipe and my crook,
If I knew of a kid that was mine."⁹

Ah, too lovely Georgiana! if sleep perchance close my eye-lids, it is
but to dream of thee.—I, for a moment, cease to feel my woes and
sorrows; nay, even think I am happy:—

"I think I press with kisses pure
Your lovely rosy lips;
And you're my bride, I think—I'm sure,
Till gold the mountain tips."¹⁰

Forgive this apostrophe, my Evelyn, it was involuntary—the name
of Georgiana acts as a charm upon me, and steals me from myself.
But to return to my farm—trees, shrubs, roots, flowers, spread
themselves profusely over its surface, and it charms in all the various, delightful, pleasing diversities of wood and water.—No other
rustic (for so I now stile myself) can boast that he possesses—

"So white a flock, so green a field."¹¹

How if Georgiana deign to accept my vows!—transporting
thought!—how if she deign to become my bride, to unite her fate
with mine; and "to travel with me hand in hand down life's steep
vale".¹²

"How if she deign my love to bless,
My fair one must not hope for dress."¹³

---

9. *Ibid.*, p. 150. The lines are:
  'Since Phillis vouchsafed me a look,
  I never once dreamt of my vine:'
10. Shenstone, 'Ode to Cynthia', *Poetical Works*, p. 148
11. Shenstone, 'Song V', *Poetical Works*, p. 172
12. Unidentified.
13. Shenstone, 'Song I', *Poetical Works*, p. 169. Correct version of line two is: 'My Flavia must
not hope for dress.'

But she will not—I know her sense—I know her mild and con-
tented, placid disposition, and beside—

> "I told my nymph, I told her true,
> My fields were small, my flocks were few."[14]

But I have trespassed too far on my Evelyn's patience; suffice it to
say that my cottage and farm contain every beauty that art or
nature can bestow, and what chiefly endears them to the heart of
Belville is that a walk of ten minutes transports him to the groves
of Belmont—the Earl too, Evelyn, as a reward for saving his
Georgiana from a ram,[15] has given me permission to sport on his
demesne, where chance may procure me an interview with the
idol of my soul.—Oh! Evelyn, rejoice with—congratulate

Your

M. BELVILLE

P.S. There is nothing like perfect happiness in this life—I have just
learned that three of my cows are in pound for trespassing on the
Vicar's glebe—unfeeling man!!

---

14. *Ibid.*, p. 168.
15. This incident is described in the following letter. Tone's use of words such as 'transport', 'tres-
    pass', 'sport', especially in connection with the 'ram', has an unmistakable sexual implication.

LETTER XV

From Lady Georgiana Shirley to Miss Juliana Blandford
BELMONT CASTLE

THE sympathetic heart of my Juliana will surely rejoice at my good fortune.—My faithful Laura has formed an acquaintance with Belville, for that is the name of the dear unknown who, "clad in humble russet grey",[1] has made such ravages in the heart of your poor Georgiana.—He is continually sauntering about the groves of Belmont, like the disconsolate shade of some unhappy lover.— She has observed him walk frequently in the dusk of evening with downcast eyes, folded arms, and irregular step.—Good heaven! how fortunate if I prove the cause of his uneasiness—adieu for a few hours—a walk round the shrubbery will give me more spirits for conversation with my Juliana.

* * *

OH! my Juliana what an escape!—blessed Providence! Oh! the gallant Belville! prodigy of strength, tenderness and courage!— Oh my Juliana what an escape!—My reflections did not allow me to perceive that I had strolled beyond the shrubbery and had got to some distance from the castle—I was suddenly roused by the apperance of a furious Ram—what could I do?—I attempted to run, but fear had fixed me to the ground—the raging animal made towards me with all its force—the fright and near approach of danger had such an immediate effect on me that I sunk into a swoon—when oh! my friend, who should appear at that moment but Belville, the lovely stranger; he saw my danger and flew like

---

1. Unidentified.

[84]

lightning to my assistance—ran between the animal and your Georgiana, seized it by the horns, and with one effort flung it over the paling into the road.

When I came to myself I found I was in the arms of my deliverer, who had used every means to recover me:—my surprise at finding myself in such a situation with my head reclined on the bosom of Belville threw me again into a swoon;—at length he brought me to myself, raised me up, and with the tenderest accents enquired after my health.—I thanked him;—he offered me the assistance of his arm—how could I in gratitude have refused it?—he ventured to press my hand—how could I have resented it?—I felt hurt at his presumption—but my heart forbad me to chide. "Sir," said I—"you have bravely saved my life at the hazard of your own"—and I presented to him my purse. "No, Madam," cried he, interrupting—"tho' I wear a peasant's garb, yet my soul is superior to my condition. I have seen better days"—and he burst into tears. "No, lovely Lady Georgiana—by assisting you, Belville is more than overpaid; all he desires is that Lady Georgiana will sometimes deign to think of one who would with pleasure lay down his life in her service—that she will not despise a person whose only happiness in life is that he has been the fortunate instrument of Lady Georgiana's preservation."

The pathetic manner in which he uttered these words, kneeling all the while, affected me extremely. "Rise, Mr. Belville," said I, stretching out my hand, which he kissed with fervour, "be assured I have too much grateful sensibility ever to forget my deliverer, one too so generous, so disinterested."—We had by this time approached the castle; Belville bowed and left me; as we parted I thought I could perceive the big tear start from his expressive eye, which seemed to say, "Adieu Lady Georgiana, your Belville doats on, adores you."

The moment I got home, I retired to my chamber and gave vent to my feelings in a flood of tears.—How I pity Belville! Pity did I say? Alas! I fear I love him. Have I not often told my Juliana how unhappy the tyrant passion would render her friend, her Georgiana? I at this moment feel a presentiment of some heavy misfortune—ah! teach his *grateful*—I am ashamed to say *doating*—Georgiana how to thank her Belville!

3 o'clock
OH! my tormented heart!—all is hurry and confusion at the castle. Mr. Belville, when he threw the raging animal into the road, overturned the Vicar's gig. The doctor threatens him with an action, which my papa has promised to defend.—Adieu—adieu—Oh! how I long for my Juliana to indulge my sorrows, and spend in her dear, dear society, a few hours of elegant distress!

GEORGIANA SHIRLEY

P.S. Sir James Dashton has composed the following elegant morceau on my escape from the Ram.—

> "Sweet-briar wounds—the rose has thorns,
> And eke, alas! the Ram has *horns*.
> But this huge *Ram* had been a *boar*,
> *If Georgiana he should gore.*"

LETTER XVI

From Montague Belville, Esq., to John Evelyn, Esq.
ELWOOD FARM

CONGRATULATE me, my dear, dear Evelyn on my unexpected good fortune. I have succeeded beyond my utmost hope—for, how could I have had the presumption to expect that I, all unworthy as I am, could have made any impression on a heart so fraught with every excellence, so replete with every accomplishment, so discerning, yet so innocent, so tender, yet so guarded, so free from suspicion, yet so fenced by natural modesty, so elegant, so perfect, so superior, yet so unpresuming as hers?—No, Evelyn, it were impossible, did not some secret divinity uphold me and lead me to that paradise I sought—that paradise where ever blooming sweets shed their enticing and chearing perfumes—where the lilly and the rose, the pink and the auricula, the geranium and carnation, the sweet-briar and violet, the hyacinth and the hare-bell, blend their various colours and each by the brightness of its own throws a lustre over the tint of the other.—The sensibility of her soul, my dear Evelyn, is only to be equalled by the graces of her person, and the enchanting softness of her manners—"Of whose person? of whose manners?"—you will exclaim. Why, whose but the lady Georgiana's? There is to me on earth no object but her. "*None*" did I say? Yes, Evelyn, *thy* friendship, *thy* goodness steals my imagination at times even from the enchanting Georgiana.

Yesterday I walked forth in despondency I know not whither; judge then of my astonishment when on passing my charmer's favourite arbour, the name of Belville pronounced by a female voice, in the accent of the Avon swan, sweetly vibrated on my ear. I stopped, listened, found I was beloved, ran and fell on my knees before her; the lively colour forsook her cheeks, her eyes closed and Georgiana fainted. A tender sympathy deprived me also, for some moments, of my faculties. I soon recovered—the situation of my angel alarmed me. What was to be done? I dare not call for assistance; nor had I any *eau de luce* in my pocket. In my eagerness and confusion I put my hand on my snuff-box, threw out the rappee, ran to the limpid rivulet, filled the box with the flowing stream and—recovered my Georgiana.—The dear angel opened her languishing eyes and thanked me with ineffable sweetness— we both dissolved into tears—at length the dinner bell rang and we must part; she smiled and bade me not despair—and when she smiled, my Evelyn, as the judicious Lee expresses it:

> "Not sea-born Venus in the courts beneath
> When the green nymphs first kissed her coral lips,
> All polished, fair and washed with orient beauty,
> Could in my dazzling fancy match her brightness."[1]

Oh! Evelyn! Georgiana must and shall be mine—I have no fortune, no attractive titles[2]—for himself alone she loves the happy Belville.—Lady Cecilia sure does not suspect my passion! but must she not—when I gaze my soul away, when my tell-tale eyes but too plainly discover what my heart would wish to conceal?—Why then do I delay to disclose to the old and venerable Earl my passion for his lovely, angelic Georgiana?—adieu—his Evelyn shall ever be nearest the heart of

M. BELVILLE

---

1. Nathaniel Lee, *The Rival Queens* (1677), III, ii.
2. Belville's position is reminiscent of Tone's, excluded from the magic circle of the landed aristocracy. See T.W. Dunne, *Theobald Wolfe Tone, Colonial Outsider: An Analysis of his Political Philosophy* (Cork, 1982), p. 15; and O. MacDonagh, *States of Mind*, p. 73.

LETTER XVII

From the Hon. C.F. Scudamore to Colonel Neville[1]
HARLEY PLACE

OH, my friend, I fear, much I fear, my weakness has ruined me.—
Twice since I last wrote to thee have I been at the Grove, but in
vain—Lady Clairville refuses, obstinately refuses to receive me.—
She is ill, dear suffering saint, and thy Scudamore sighs in all the
anguish of sympathetic sorrow.—Alas, I am the cause, the unhappy cause of her calamity.—Clairville too, the monster, maltreats
her.[2]—What shall I do? Good angels, guard my love!—Oh my
heart, my agonizing heart!—curse on this woman's weakness.

Last night I again attempted to gain admission at the Grove,
but, alas, without success.—As I returned, my steps were involun-
tarily led to the spot where I had the happiness to preserve the
invaluable life of my Eliza. A thousand tender ideas came crowd-
ing in my soul; the sky was clear, the azure vault was spangled with
myriads of stars, which, as we are told in the sacred volume of
Truth, "run their course rejoicing".[3] The moon in maiden modesty arose, and shed a silver light over the solemn scene; all nature
was serene, I looked up to heaven, the tears flowed down my
cheeks. Alas, thought I, why was I born? Why sent into this breath-
ing world? What is the world to me without my love? And she, Oh,
misery! Oh, distraction! disdains me. Cruel Eliza!—unpitying
stars, ye shine as bright as though my love were kind; the moon
too has arisen in cloudless majesty, as much composed as though
my soul were calm.—See her bright face unmoved; the beasts, the

---

1. In the NLI copy at this point, the printer's error 'Belville' has been corrected in pen to 'Neville'.
2. Tone insisted that Martin neglected his wife by his frequent absences from home. See *Humanity Dick*, pp. 45–54.
3. Judges 5.20.

birds too are retired to rest, and all the functions of nature are exercised in the ordinary *routine*, regardless of my miseries. Oh, Heavens! Oh, earth! Oh, seas! Oh, skies! bear witness to my sorrows; and ye chaste stars,[4] answer, if in your nocturnal revolution ye have, with rays beneficent, glimmered on the griefs of such a wretch as Scudamore!

My fancy could not sustain the picture of misery which my reason had drawn, and I sunk down on the verdant greensward in an agony of despair. "Yes, my Eliza," I exclaimed, "we shall meet both here and hereafter—we shall know one another again"—and I hung my pensive head,[5] meditating on futurity and the transmigration of souls.

Suddenly the scene was changed, the clouds gathered, and in an instant burst on my defenceless head in cataracts of rain; the hoarsely bellowing thunder muttered out discontent; the vivid glare of the brisk lightning flashed forth indignation; I was wet to the skin, but what of that—

> "——The tempest in my mind
> Did from my senses take all feeling else,
> Save what beat there."[6]

"It is well," I cried, "this jarring conflict of the elements, faint emblem of the discordant passions which rend my heart, suits well with the gloomy habit of my soul—but Oh! the unhappy mariners, exposed to the pelting of this pitiless storm,[7] how shall they bear it, when the laboring bark[8] climbs the foamy surge as high as to the heavens, and ducks again as low as to the shades of Tartarus.— Yes, gallant seamen, for you I feel"—and my cheeks were again suffused with briny torrents!—but my passion for Eliza has rendered me but too sensible of the sorrows of mothers—pity the *foiblesse* of my heart—I am as weak as a child.

---

4. *Othello*, V, ii, 2.
5. Milton, *Lycidas*, l, 146.
6. *King Lear*, I, iv, 11.
7. *Ibid.*, III, iv, 29.
8. *Othello*, II, i, 89.

All this while I stood on the common exposed, defenceless, to the rage of the elements.—I stood unmoved, unfeeling, as if I had forgot myself to stone. To soothe my sorrows and calm the tempest of my mind, I took out of my pocket (which I always carry about me) a patent flute of Potter's, with the additional keys[9]—I touched the instrument, which vibrated on my ear in sympathetic sorrow, strains suited to my state:

"Water parted from the sea."[10]

And, the heavenly air of the divine Jackson:

"For ever Fortune wilt thou prove,
An unrelenting foe to me."[11]

"Cruel Fortune," I exclaimed, unscrewing my flute, and putting it again into my pocket, "when will thy malice have an end?"—and I burst into tears.

But here I was interrupted by the arrival of my chariot, which my trusty Williams[12] had prepared and brought forth in quest of me.—I suffered myself to be conducted back to Harley Place, where I found a chicken boiled for my supper and a blazing wood fire in the chimney. Shall I confess it to you, my friend, spite of my feelings, spite of my love for Eliza, I changed my clothes, eat my chicken, and drank a flask of Burgundy after it. And can angelic

---

Richard Potter, a well-known flute-maker, adopted new keys on the flute, made about 1774, on which Vanhall performed at the Hague, and which Potter later sold to Asher, the Irish flautist. In 1785 Potter took out the first English patent for improvements on the flute. They included seven keys (in order to obtain all the semitones), a metal tuning slide, a screw cork in the head joint and conical metal valves on the keys. He made no claim to having invented these improvements; they were all known previously. See F.J. Crowest (ed.), *The Story of the Flute* (London, 1914), p. 43.

). A once well-known song by Thomas Arne from the opera *Artaxerxes* (1762), which was performed with great success at the Crow Street Theatre in 1765, when it was sung by the great tenor Tenducci. See T.J. Walsh, *Opera in Dublin*, p. 141.

. From William Jackson's opera *The Lord of the Manor* (1781), Act V, I; performed in Crow Street Theatre that year.

. Williams later betrays Scudamore in a letter to Lord Clairville. This parallels the involvement of Richard Martin's servant, Joseph, in delivering a letter to Lady Vesey from her husband and of witnessing and reporting the disregard with which she received it. See *Humanity Dick*, p. 77.

purity, my love, forgive such gross sensuality? Thou who art purity itself!—impossible. Yet thou art good and tender as thou art beautiful—still will I hope for thy forgiveness, and in the awful hour of dissolution, that dear reflection shall soothe my sorrow and calm the agonies of my soul in her departing moments!

With grief I find, my friend, that the frail machine which wraps me, the prison of my soul, is unequal to these flights of sensibility.—I am, to-day, confined to my chamber with a violent sore throat and swelled jaw; my voice is scarce audible, and I am so enveloped in flannel that, between my love and this disguise, thou wouldst hardly know thy Scudamore; but whatever cruel change Destiny may inflict on my outward form, my heart is still the same, and tells me in silent accents, that I am

And ever shall be
My dear Neville's[1]
Most affectionate friend
The unhappy
C.F. SCUDAMORE

---

13. 'Belville' printed here instead of 'Neville'.

LETTER XVIII

From Lady Georgiana Shirley to Miss Juliana Blandford
BELMONT CASTLE

OH! my dearest Juliana, what a discovery!—give me joy a thousand times. Belville has *confessed* to me he loves me, with a passion still more violent, if possible, than mine for him.—Strange! you will say, that Belville, that hitherto timid, respectful Belville, the youth who sighed at humble distance, should have dared to *confess* a passion for your lovely Georgiana!—not quite so surprising, my dear—but list.

Yesterday the weather was remarkably warm, and I had given orders for my *piano forte* to be removed to my favourite arbour, where Georgiana and her lovely Juliana have passed away so many pleasing hours of sensibility and innocence.—Thither I retired to enjoy the cooling breeze and think on Belville—the pleasing solitude of this delightful, sequestered and romantic spot; the united odours of roses and jessamine and eglantine; the warbling of birds; and the soft murmuring of a limpid rivulet, which you remember runs close to this enchanting bower[1]—all, all conspired to throw me into the most agreeable lassitude and pleasing dejection of spirits.

Alas! said I to myself—how hard is the fate of wretched, wretched Georgiana!—Ye little warblers: you are not restrained by tyrant custom from whispering your pure and innocent loves to the object of your choice!—You have no rigid, cruel parents to force or restrain your inclinations; but free as the air, your kindred element, you hop from spray to spray accompanied by the

---

Rosamund's bower was a marked architectural feature of Charlemont's demesne at Marino. See Maurice Craig, *The Volunteer Earl* (London, 1948), p. 123.

charming partners of your cares and affections—bathe in the same rivulet—and when the descending sun warns you of night's approach, you retreat in chearful, endearing innocence to the same pendent cottage, and repose like our first parents on the same downy pillow.

Here the reflection of my sorrows overcame me—and I sat some minutes, with my head reclined on my hand, dissolved in tears.—Oh! my friend, how would you have pitied your Georgiana! how would the sympathetic tear have glistened in my Juliana's eye! At length, ashamed of my weakness, I, after a violent effort, in some measure recovered myself—rose up and walked with trembling step towards the *piano forte*—sat down, and began with the most lively expression that soothing strain, which, I told you, I had composed on my passion for the too charming Belville:

> AIR I
> My tender, too sensible heart
> Throbs quick when my Belville is near;
> But, alas! when he strives to depart,
> My soft cheek is bedewed with a tear.
>
> II
> Thus the rose, when mild Zephyr appears
> With emotion inclines its sweet head;
> And the dew-drops resemble my tears—
> See—the rose with weeping is red.
>
> III
> I am like the soft down on the peach,
> And Belville the insect within—
> The juicy ripe *heart* he can reach,
> But leaves its sweet bloom to the *skin*.

My tears, dearest Juliana, flowed with such unceasing rapidit towards the cadence of the last verse that they prevented me from seeing Belville, who had during the symphony stolen into th arbour with the soft and silent step of love. Judge then of my fee ings, my dear, my amiable friend, when I beheld the lovely yout at my feet, bathed in tears and pressing my hand with all th enthusiastic fervor of the tenderest raptures!—His touch thrilled to my soul—I sighed—breathed short—and fainted away.—When I came to myself, I found the terrified Belville, who was by this time recovered (for he also had fallen into a swoon), still at my feet, and bathed in tears.—"Ah!" cried he, in the softest, tenderest accents—"do I behold my Georgiana revive?—do I once more see the carnation resume its empire over her cheek—the coral blush upon her pouting lip, and the beam of love, innocence and beauty glisten in her eye?—I do—Georgiana revives, and I am happy!"

I remained all this time in a state of the utmost confusion—I was ready to sink at the thought of the discovery I had made;—"Rise, Sir," said I faintly, and striving to disengage my hand—"you have meanly intruded on my privacy and learned the secret of my heart; but know sir," said I, raising my voice, "my partiality for you is not so violent, but I can resent your intrusion, and make Mr. Belville as much the object of my hatred and aversion as, I am weak enough to confess, he has been that of my esteem and perhaps of"—my tears and confusion stopped my utterance.—"Charming, angelic creature, lovely, enchanting Lady Georgiana," cried he, in mournful accents, still holding my hand in his, "do not, do not fly me!—pardon the rudeness of my intrusion; pardon your Belville who adores you—chance alone brought me here—chance then alone should incur my Georgiana's displeasure"—and he burst into tears. His tears moved me—how could I see my Belville "kneel at my feet and sigh to be forgiven"?—"Sir," replied I—"your apology is sufficient and for this time I pardon you"—he seized my hand and almost devoured it with kisses;—"Enchanting goodness," cried he, "oh happy intrusion! oh fortunate discovery!—now, now Fate I defy thy malice!—my Georgiana, that dear, enchanting idol of my soul, does not, does not hate me."—At that moment the bell rang as a summons to dinner.—"Leave me, Sir," cried I hastily.—"What, leave you Lady Georgiana," exclaimed he—"and in this dreadful uncertainty of despair!" "Sir," replied I, with a smile—"the coward alone *despairs*."—A beam of joy and gratitude shot over his countenance; he kissed my hand with rapture—flew across the lawn and was out of sight in a moment.

With a thousand mixed emotions I moved slowly toward the

castle—adieu, my dear, how I long for your friendly bosom to repose on.—My Father sure will never consent to my union with a person so much below me in birth and fortune as Mr. Belville—all is doubt—fear and distraction—adieu!—adieu!

GEORGIANA SHIRLEY

LETTER XIX

From the Hon. C.F. Scudamore to Colonel Neville
PORTLAND PLACE

YOU will doubtless, Colonel, be a little surprised at the date of this letter; but that scoundrel Clairville has by some vile means or other imbibed a suspicion of my attachment to his wife, and in an instant hurried her up to Portman Square. I flew after them on the wings of love and rapturous expectation, and have sat at home, *perdue*,[1] coiled up like an animated serpent, meditating mischief for this fortnight.—I have imps employed to watch the door of Clairville's house, and learn from them that her Ladyship never stirs out.—I know her attachment to the pleasures of London, and am therefore well convinced that the brute, her husband, restrains her liberty.—Gods! Ye mighty Gods! And shall such things be? Alas! my Eliza! why cannot I fly with thee to some desert wide and wild[2]—there where no Clairvilles reign, press thee to my panting heart, and revel on thy beauties, unviewed by all, save the eye of the guardian angels who, recording our transports, would drop a tear of pity on the book, and blot them away for ever!

But ah, my friend, such bliss is denied to thy unhappy Scudamore—all day, all night I rave of nought but my Eliza. My head is unsettled—tears dim my eyes—I scarce know what I write.

* * *

Yesterday morning I came down to breakfast with only one stocking on, and without my *Robe de chambre*.—I poured the coffee into the sugar-bowl, and emptied the cream ewer into a caddie of gun-

---

. Adapted from the French military phrase *sentinelle perdue*, meaning 'in a very advanced and dangerous position'. This meaning is enforced by the subsequent reference to the serpent.
. *Venice Preserv'd*, I, I.

powder tea. My faithful William's patience is almost exhausted with my extravagancies.—Mirror of domestics! thy services shall not go unrewarded or forgotten. He brought me my other stocking and my gown—I suffered him to put them on, sitting myself all the time, like Patience on a monument smiling at grief,[3] and insensible of his assiduities. But ah, my friend! what is exterior? what is dress?—oh, Eliza! Eliza!

Think not, however, that my own miseries so completely fill my soul, but that in one corner there is still room to sympathize with thee.—But, alas, thou art not formed like me—those denials and difficulties but arouse your spirit which would sink me into the gloomy abyss of dark despair.—Yet, by heaven, I will not suffer alone!—No!—here I give my foolish dejection to the viewless winds![4] Avaunt my fears and now for the enterprise.

> "And damned be he that first cries—hold, enough!"[5]

Yes, Colonel, thy friend will once more be himself, no longer the humble, desponding slave of this dear, dear—I durst not write her name, lest before the magic all my frail resolves should vanish into air.

Lord Clairville, I learn from my spy, is constantly at Lady Middleton's, who is likewise in town, and frequently remains *tête-à-tête* with her ladyship till four in the morning.[6]—A thought occurs—

> "Oh glorious thought!—by heaven I will enjoy it,
> Tho' but in fancy."[7]

What it is, you must be ignorant till my next.—I fly to execute it—adieu, my Neville—wish me success.

Yours as ever—
C.F. SCUDAMORE

3. *Twelfth Night*, II, iv, 117.
4. *Measure for Measure*, III, i, 124.
5. *Macbeth*, V, viii, 33. Cf. Tone's diary, 26 February 1796.
6. Tone was known to stay in Lady Vesey's company until this hour. Given the known and lurid details of Lady Vesey's conduct with Mr Petrie, this is a comic euphemism.
7. Unidentified.

LETTER XX

From Lady Georgiana Shirley to Miss Juliana Blandford
BELMONT CASTLE

MY affection for my dearest Juliana has suggested to my bosom a thousand excuses for her long silence—the horrid account of your danger, in the letter of which my brother was the bearer, and which was the last I received, raises a thousand glaring phantoms in my breast;—and my imagination pictures you, perhaps sinking under the brutal violence of some lawless ruffian or parched by febrile heat, occasioned by the agitation of my Juliana's spirits. Do my sweet, my amiable friend, take up your pen but for a moment, and give ease to the apprehensive soul of your Georgiana—tell her you return her amiable brother's affection and that you will enable your Georgiana to stile you by a more endearing appellation.—Apropos—I believe that whimsical being, Sir James Dashton, is enamoured of my sister Cecilia;—he pays her the most marked attention, and she—you know her passion for flirtation—contrives to have him continually at her heels.—Whenever she sees him approach, she pretends to avoid him and runs into the wood or shrubbery, whither Sir James literally *dances* after her, and on an hour's search, perhaps all the while *sans chapeau*, returns to the castle out of breath, where my laughing sister had arrived long before. He gets numerous falls to which Cecilia encourages him, by pretending to entertain doubts of his activity; and whenever we ride an airing, she switches his spirited horse, which immediately runs off with him, to the great entertainment of our little party.

We rode yesterday to Elwood races, where my giddy sister contrived to set off Sir James's horse amongst the crowds of carriages on the course; and Sir James had been inevitably killed had not my Belville sprung from his saddle like lightning and seized the animal by the bridle, at the hazard of his life.—Belville at that moment appeared to me in so amiable a light, that I could not restrain myself from breaking out into an exclamation in his praise—but luckily my sister, who sometimes rallies me on my rustic admirer, was too much interested in Sir James's safety to attend to what I said. Sir James was in raptures with my swain, and thanked him in the most extravagant manner, nay absolutely insisted on his riding back to our groupe, where he received the thanks and compliments of my papa, the other gentlemen, and Cecilia;—he returned their politeness by a most graceful bow— said he deserved no praise for any attentions he had the honour of paying the Shirley family, and at the same time darted at your Georgiana a glance so expressive of tenderness and love as penetrated to my very soul.—My papa insisted on his accompanying us to dinner at the castle, which he modestly declined, thro' a fear, as I could discern by his expressive eyes, of giving even a moment's uneasiness to his Georgiana.

All the way home we talked of indifferent matters—all seemed charmed with my Belville's conversation except Colonel Neville, in whose eye lurked jealousy and aversion. Oh! my Juliana, how I dread that monster—adieu—think on Mortimer—think on—

GEORGIANA SHIRLEY

LETTER XXI

From Lord Mortimer to John Evelyn, Esq.
BELMONT CASTLE

RESTORED as I am to my family and my friends, surrounded by every thing that the most capacious mind could wish for, yet, my Evelyn, am I far from happy.—The idea of the too lovely Juliana still disturbs my peace. Too justly didst thou prophecy, my friend, my heart, which for these three years withstood the attacks of all that France or Italy could boast of, is at length subdued.[1] Do not think, however, I am ashamed of my defeat; no, I glory in the chains of my Juliana—"my Juliana", did I say?—Oh, Evelyn! that such I could call her—but thou knowest the foible of my father; noble as is his character and partial as I am to it, yet must I admit and lament that haughty pride which, however it may often be the parent of virtue, is as frequently productive of the most unhappy errors. Never, Evelyn, never would he consent to an alliance with Juliana; his fond partiality for his son assures him that I shall add to the splendor of our family; the proudest of our peers, he thinks, might be honored by an union with me; and severe indeed would be his disappointment to behold me married to one whose family, however exalted her merits, has been contaminated by trade.—My amiable sisters have none of these scruples; they perceive my passion; the sprightly Cecilia rallies me upon it, she says she knows I am too dutiful to marry without the Earl's consent, and thinks the best way is for us both to die for love, it will make so charming a subject for a novel. My lovely Georgiana sympathizes with me, and as she corresponds with my Juliana, I have the consolation of gazing on her writing and imprinting a thousand kisses on her adored name.

---

1. Lord Charlemont travelled extensively abroad, including visits to France and Italy.

Poor Georgiana! I am afraid she is a fellow-sufferer.—Belville whom, I believe, you know, has taken a farm near the castle; he is become intimate in the family—most eminently does he possess all the virtues of the heart, and seldom have I found such abilities so highly polished.—The inequality of his fortune, however, will, I am afraid, in my father's mind, be an eternal bar to their union; though never were there two hearts so adapted to each other by nature.

Sir James Dashton, who is at present at the castle, is a fund of entertainment to us; he certainly is enamoured of Cecilia, though that sly girl will not let me see whether the flame burns with reciprocal violence—I must own I should not be concerned if a match was to take place; for Dashton, though he is such a coxcomb, has certainly a good heart, and the sprightly humour of Cecilia is the best adapted to rally him out of his absurdities. His passion makes him more ridiculous than ever.—He has got a phaeton of the most extravagant height, and he drives six horses with such rashness that I am really afraid of his neck; he has already got half a dozen falls, but luckily the only consequence was a great deal of mirth at his expence. Not content, however, with his present phaeton, he told us the other day that he had bespoke one as high again, and lamented that the etiquette was for none but the king to have more than six horses, or, he assured us, he would drive eight in hand. He likes the prince's character very well, but then, sir, he seldom goes beyond a gig or a curricle.—As for Pitt, he may be a good statesman, but—he can't drive.—Notwithstanding these extravagancies, Sir James has many excellent points.—His understanding is naturally an excellent one; and the same vanity which makes him wish to be at the head of the fashion had an admirable effect in carrying him through his studies, and there are few branches of learning and few polite accomplishments in which he does not make a distinguished figure.—This desire of universal pre-eminence is productive of a thousand curious circumstances; Doctor Clarges,[2] whose deep learning you are no stranger to,

2. This name might derive from Clarges Street in London, where Lady Vesey's brother had a house, to which she eloped with Mr Petrie.

dined the other day at the castle. Sir James, whose dress on that day was peculiarly extravagant, with surprising volubility had entertained us during the whole time of dinner with a dissertation upon driving; to this succeeded an account of the new method of handling cocks;[3] he informed us of a receipt possessed, and indeed invented, by his Frenchman for making pearl powder;[4] and he concluded with a panegyric on the inventor of patent stockings.—The Doctor listened to his rhapsodies with good-humoured patience, but after dinner he entered into a conversation with my father upon a late publication on the laws of motion; such a coxcomb as Sir James he imagined would be obliged to listen with submissive silence, but what was his surprise to find him possessed of the same fluency of words on a philosophical subject as he had displayed on the former ones: and possessed of the same desire of pre-eminence, whether in establishing the orthodoxy of a disputed reading or claiming the invention of a fashionable button.—But these levities, Evelyn, can but for a moment divert my thoughts from their adored object.—Thy presence perhaps might in some measure tend to alleviate my sufferings; when am I to hope for it?

When will your affairs in Yorkshire be so settled as to let you give some time to your friends? Of them all, my dear Evelyn, it is needless to say, there is none more sincerely yours, than

MORTIMER

3. Goold had a reputation for gambling and for various dubious sporting activities. See Curran, *Sketches of the Irish Bar*, pp. 185ff.
4. A cosmetic used to whiten the skin.

LETTER XXII

From Miss Juliana Blandford to Lady Georgiana Shirley
GROSVENOR SQUARE

MY dearest Georgiana's last letter has affected me with various emotions—mirth at the character of Sir James Dashton, so humourously drawn; pity for the doating Belville; but on what you say of me, oh, my Georgiana! can you then think that such would be my return for all the favours conferred on me by your family? Lord Mortimer!—oh, heavens, the accomplished, noble Mortimer! The representative of that ancient house—no, my Georgiana—tell him not to cast a thought on the unhappy Juliana, tell him she would perish rather than disappoint the high hopes of his doating family; tell him that grandeur is not the ambition of Juliana, but that on him it is incumbent to support the honour of his house—to extend the lustre of his name; his friends will expect, and justly expect, some great alliance, some splendid connexion—and would you have me be so meanly selfish as to contribute to the downfall of these high hopes? No, my Georgiana, I know my own heart, and never, never shalt thou have room to accuse me.—But I hear Lady Fillamar calling me to attend her to the opera; some business which occupied me the whole morning prevented me from sitting down earlier to converse with my Georgiana,[1] and as I will not let a post pass without giving you even a few lines, I am obliged to close this. May Fortune ever be propitious to my Georgiana, are the wishes of her

Unalterably affectionate
JULIANA BLANDFORD

1. The NLI text here misprinted 'Juliana' for 'Georgiana'.

LETTER XXIII

From the Hon. C.F. Scudamore to Colonel Neville

"I thought of dying, better things appear"[1]—yes, Colonel, congratulate, felicitate me;—my Eliza, for *mine* I may now call her, is kind, and I am happy.

"Blest as the immortal Gods is *he*![2]

(Plague on it, it should be *I*) and now,

"My soul hath her content so absolute
That not another moment like to this,
Succeeds in unknown fate!"[3]

Damn your quotations, methinks I hear you cry, what in the devil's name does all this rhodomontade[4] lead to?—lead, my friend?—to bliss, to transport, to rapture, to Lady Clairville (there is a climax for you!)—Oh, my soul's idol, my heart's treasure, my charmer!—I have been quaffing Burgundy to her dear health till my head reels like a smoke-jack,[5] and my heart flames like Mount-Ætna, or the face of Lady ——.* But she is mine, the dear, dear enchanting lovely angel—no, not yet—not absolutely, literally *mine*, but tomorrow night—Gods!—

---

1. Unidentified.
2. Ambrose Philips, *Fragments of Sappho*, 1709. See *Poems*, ed. M.G. Segar (Oxford, 1937).
3. *Othello*, II, i, 193.
4. A vainglorious piece of bragging or boasting; derived from the braggart Moorish king Rodomonte in Ariosto's *Orlando Furioso*.
5. An apparatus for turning a roasting-spit. It is fixed in a chimney and set in motion by the current of air.
* The Editor chooses, for good reasons, to suppress the name of the lady alluded to.

"Venus, be thou tomorrow great"—[6]

Yes, my friend, tomorrow night surrenders, unconditionally, the loveliest, fairest, kindest of her sex to the triumphant arms of thy happy Scudamore.

Last night, when the pale moon and silent stars shone, conscious of my ingenuity, I put on a livery which I had bespoke in exact imitation of Lord Clairville's (by the bye I made a devilish smart footman); and at eleven o'clock, when my spy informed me his Lordship was housed at Lady Middleton's, I set out to Portman Square, knocked at the door; the porter, who was drunk, admitted me without suspicion, and I desired to be shewn to Lady Clairville, having a message to deliver from his Lordship.—I knew Clairville was fast for four hours at least.—My scheme succeeded to a miracle. I was sent into the drawing room where her Ladyship sat alone in her night dress. Good Gods, such a figure! such eyes! such hair! such teeth! but all this I have told you of before.—Well—I ran over to her, threw myself at her feet, seized her snowy hand and pressed it to my lips. "Oh, my Lady Clairville," cried I in transport, "can you forgive the innocent stratagem which love, the tyrant deity before whom all mortals bow, and immortals also, inspires?"—"Sir," says the dear lovely fair one, "this is very extraordinary behaviour.—I hoped that the stern repulse which rigid virtue dictated, had stifled in the bud those presumptuous hopes, that like another Phaeton with daring head would seize the glowing chariot of the sun!—Begone, for ever quit my presence, nor with your impious passion shock mine ears, else will I this very moment, spite of your prayers, your tears and protestations, ring for my footmen and have you expelled with ignominy from the house!"—What could I do, my friend?—I saw her lovely eyes kindle with indignation, and she held, majestically, her ivory finger on the spring of the bell. I instantly drew forth my pistols from my right hand coat-pocket, for I had brought a case for the nonce[7] (not loaded indeed for fear of

---

6. Unidentified.
7. Tone was temporarily barred from Trinity College because of a duelling incident in which he had been a second. Richard Martin was renowned for his duelling and for the tenacity with which he pursued his opponent to take up the challenge.

accidents, my pistols not having stops to the cocks) and exclaimed in piteous accents, "Oh, Werter, Werter what a soul was thine!—Come, death!—come, grim king of terrors!—come to a wretch's aid!—ease at once the weight of misery under which I groan—come! oh come!"—All this while the dear angel, I suppose from apprehension, remained fixed at the fireside, looking earnestly to see what would follow.—"And will you, my Eliza," I exclaimed, "behold my death?—will she see those eyes closed in eternal night,[8] which pant but to look on her?—will she, unpitying, doom her Scudamore to despair and certain destruction?"—Finding her still fixed as a statue, in an agony I drew my other pistol from my left hand coat-pocket, and cocking it sat down on the sofa. "Thus then," I cried, "I bid a long adieu to a life of sorrow"; and applying the muzzle of one to my right ear, I had the supreme felicity to hear my charmer exclaim—"Cruel Mr. Scudamore! would you then shoot yourself in my presence?"—"My angel," I cried, flinging away the pistols and flying to her feet, "do you then wish me to live?—now indeed is my life of value in my eyes, since my Eliza deigns to cast away one thought on its preservation; yes, my fair, for thy dear sake I will take all imaginable care of it, and every moment of my future existence shall be devoted to thy service!"—I saw the soft emotion of tenderness beam from her radiant eyes, and was determined to follow my blow.—"To-morrow night," I exclaimed, "my angel, the club at Almacks[9] give a superb masquerade—behold this ticket!—see on the paper how the magic pencil of *Cipriani*,[10] aided by the creative graver of *Bartolozzi*,[11] has pourtrayed the goddess of pleasure, peeping with laughter-loving eyes thro' her masque—behold

---

8. *Richard III*, V, iii, 62.
9. Named after the original proprietor in 1765. It was opened with a 10-guinea subscription for which there was a ball and a supper once a week for twelve weeks.
10. Italian decorative painter and designer who came to London in 1755 and was a founder member of the Royal Academy. He was famous for architectural details like plasterwork, woodwork and stonecarving. In this respect he served Charlemont, of whom he was a personal friend. (Craig, *Volunteer Earl*, p. 155.)
11. Engraver to George III. He popularized the stipple process and reproduced works by Cipriani using this technique. He lived in intimacy with Lord Charlemont, whom he admired for his literary attainments. 'Bartollozi would fain engrave the picture before it is sent to you.' (*Ibid.*)

at her knee a little cupid whose lips an emblematic bandage binds; that bandage which grosser spirits have transferred to his eyes—see this emblem explained in choice Italian, *Muto, non cieco, Mute, not blind*!—and can the soft hand of my Eliza withstand all this?"—"No, Scudamore," she cried, "I can be no longer insensible to your passion, nor shall thy tenderness go unrewarded—Lady Clairville may perhaps be cruel, but to-morrow evening at the Pantheon in Oxford-street,[12] if thou shouldst meet a rustic nymph, clad in a white jacket, trimmed with a vestris[13] blue, she may perhaps listen to thy vows"—here a loud knocking at the door interrupted our conversation—"'tis my Lord," exclaimed Lady Clairville, "and if he sees you I am ruined."—"Fear not, my angel," I cried, "for I shall descend by the back stairs"—then seizing her lovely hand I devoured it with kisses and withdrew undiscovered.

On my way home my joy was so great, my transports so violent that, absorbed in reverie, I ran full against a chimney sweeper and overset him. The fellow rose instantly from the kennel, and damning the blind eyes of Scudamore, struck me on the face—my choler rose, and I, forgetting my rank and assuming the manners as well as the garb of a footman, returned the blow—a scuffle ensued which terminated in a *boxing match*.[14]—The mob having formed a ring we stripped and *set to*—my antagonist stood up very fairly, and *stopped* several of my best blows with considerable dexterity and skill; but at length, thanks to the kind instructions of the immortal Mendoza,[15] the tutor of thy friend in the gymnastic science, *I put in*

---

12. Theatre and public promenade, opened January 1772. Mrs Delany writes: 'I hear a great deal of the magnificence and elegance of the Pantheon in Oxford Road ... I suppose Almacks and Soho must hide their diminished heads.' The masque that took place there the following month was the one in which 'the quadrille of the new order of monks' became the topic of fashionable conversation. The service there had deteriorated by 1788. See Ashton, *Old Times*, p. 215.

13. Opera singer then in vogue. Her name was later adopted by Eliza Lucy Bartollozi (1797–1806), famous in the 1830s. See *The Revels History of Drama in English* VI (London, 1975), p. 131. Women often played male roles—like Macheath in *The Beggar's Opera*—wearing breeches trimmed with 'vestris' blue. See T.J. Walsh, *Opera in Dublin*, p. 128.

14. The phrase was first used by Addison in *The Spectator*, no. 5 (1714).

15. A Jewish boxer and champion of England. 'Mendoza's terms are reasonable enough—eight lessons for a guinea.' (Ashton, *Old Times*, p. 274.)

a straightblow just under the left ear of the sooty hero, which upset him instantly in the mud, and spread a momentary stupor over all his faculties—on this he *gave in* and allowed thy now victorious friend to be the better man. But ah, my Neville, what is victory? what is fame? The blooming laurels of thy Scudamore are disgraced by a "*dusky circle*"[16] which invelopes hisright eye.—The vanquished chimney-sweeper called the watch—I attempted to bribe the villains, but found to my ineffable confusion that the gentleman who had been my second in the combat had rewarded himself for this exertion of friendship with my watch and purse.—What was to be done?—I *charged* my adversary in my turn, and we were led off to the round house.[17] On my arrival there I sent for my shoemaker, who instantly bailed me out, and at his intercession I forgave the sweep.

As I wear a masque tomorrow night, I am in hopes that Lady Clairville may not discover the *derangement* of my eye. For this purpose I shall assume the motley garb of an Harlequin, as his masque covers the whole head.—Adieu, my friend!—I have scribbled a volume.—Wish me success—either fortune is basely my enemy, or to-morrow night makes me the happiest of men—*Io triumphe! Raptures and Paradise!*[18]—Venus and the Graces!—

"Lutes, laurels, seas of milk, and ships of amber!"[19]

C.F. SCUDAMORE

---

16. Unidentified.
17. Gaol.
18. Unidentified.
19. Otway, *Venice Preserv'd* V, i. 369.

LETTER XXIV

From Lady Georgiana Shirley to Miss Juliana Blandford
BELMONT CASTLE

MY father's cruel obstinacy, and Colonel Neville's tiresome and odious passion, have at last compelled me to a step—a precipice—at the sight of which a few weeks since my blood had run cold.— To avoid being forced to marry a man I hate and detest, I have consented this night to elope with Belville—*elope*—I dread even to write the word—what terror, then, must not the act itself raise in my bosom?—Yes, my Juliana, to elope with a person almost a stranger to me!—what will the world say of me? how will a malicious, talking world censure your Georgiana?—but I care not, the world to me is my constant, faithful, amiable, dear, dear, Belville, and my friend, my lovely Juliana. Yes, my Juliana, secure of thy friendship and my Belville's love I could roam with pleasure over the sandy deserts of Arabia.

> "Hear unappall'd the tawny lion's roar,
> And bellowing tygers rage along the shore!"

Renounce every delicacy of life, imagine the infrequent spring my tokay, and the wild berry my venison—the whistling of the unpitying wind around my defenceless head, *accompanied* by the soft accents of my friend, would be to me the softest music; and if I once longed for an habitation it should be that I might shelter Belville and my Juliana from the rude indecencies of the weather.—Advise me, my friend, what to do!—*Elope*—this night!—Oh! my palpitating heart—nine o'clock!—adieu—my lovely friend—pity—think on your

GEORGIANA SHIRLEY

P.S. The following lines I found hung on my favourite tree this morning.

> "Go! scroll, my Georgiana tell
> How much I love her, and how well!
> Go, scroll, and whisper in her ear
> Her love, her faithful Belville's near;
> Tell her, if by pale Cynthia's light
> She'll meet her true love here tonight,
> That without ripening sun or shower
> Pansies shall blow in half an hour;
> Beneath her foot the rose shall bloom
> *Without* its *thorn* but *with perfume*,
> The pink, the violet, and gilly—
> Flower shall arise, and eke the lilly:
> Go, *faithful* scroll, and to her view
> Recall her doating Montague."

Oh! Juliana, are they not tenderly elegant!

LETTER XXV

From Montague Belville, Esq., to John Evelyn, Esq.
ELWOOD FARM

ADIEU, my Evelyn!—I am the happiest of mortals—Georgiana, the dear angel, has consented to be mine—this happy night at the hour of ten gives my charmer to her longing Belville—adieu, my friend—at the Shrubbery she meets me!—I shall have a chaise prepared!—Then, "Fortune, I defy thee!"[1]—Once more, adieu!— I am all joy, rapture and expectation in the extreme. Adieu!—to hope for the Earl, her father's consent, were madness.—Adieu, adieu!

Ten o'clock!—the chaise is ready—my throbbing heart tells me it is time.

Once more, my friend, adieu!—adieu!—

M. BELVILLE

---

1. Possibly a modernized form of Chaucer's 'For fynally, Fortune, I thee defye!', the refrain of the first of his balades on Fortune, *Le Pleintif countre Fortune.*

LETTER XXVI

From Colonel Neville to the Hon. C.F. Scudamore
BELMONT CASTLE

BRAVO! Scudamore, bravissimo!—thou dost business with a vengeance—thou must have the eyes of a basilisk to make that haughty fair one Lady Clairville drop like a ripened peach into your arms.—Last week you were dying with despair, and now you proudly sing "*Io triumphe*". This night you feast on beauty—this night too your Neville riots in the charms of Georgiana.—Yes, my friend, my Fitzroy—this night your Neville leads her far from Belmont, and *forces* the cruel tyrant beauty to her happiness. List to my plot!—am I not a precious villain?—It is true, I am, but love and revenge at once agitate my furious soul and overcome my weaker reason. Lady Georgiana has, this night, agreed to *elope* with Belville; he has assumed the disguise of a peasant more effectually to cloak his design.[1] I have intercepted a letter of Lady Georgiana's to him appointing the time, place, and signal—this letter have I forwarded to that Belville, but altered the hour of meeting. At nine, veiled in the dusk of night, I carry off my Georgiana—and at ten I have so contrived that Belville shall mistake my Sultana, Lucy, for his Georgiana.—Then my Scudamore, shall I feast on ambrosia, and clasp the delicious angel to this panting bosom!—Congratulate your Neville—when I have triumphed over my Georgiana's virtue, to escape the censure of the malicious world she must consent to be my wife.

Adieu—I fly to my charmer—

---

1. When eloping with Mr Petrie, Lady Vesey dressed as a peasant-cum-harlot and set off in a series of coaches to meet her lover.

"Oh! this night,
Or either makes us, or undoes us quite."[2]

HENRY NEVILLE

2. *Othello*, V, i, 128.

LETTER XXVII

From Lady Myrtilla Middleton to Lord Clairville
WELBECK STREET

MY dear Lord,

Read the inclosed, and if you have one spark of honour, if you would avoid the name of credulous, wittol husband,[1] you know your course.—Ask not how I came by this intelligence, but act as becomes Lord Clairville, if ever you hope again for happiness in the arms of yours, as ever,

M. MIDDLETON

[Enclosed in the foregoing]

TO LADY MIDDLETON.

MADAM,

The many kindnesses I have received from your Ladyship bind me so strongly to your commands that I feel it my duty to let you know that my master is to meet my Lady Clairville this night, at the masquerade, from whence they propose adjourning to a certain house in Soho, kept by one ——: I am to be there, and have everything prepared.—In pursuance of your commands, I think it proper to acquaint you of this,

And am, madam,
Your Ladyship's
Very humble servant,
WILLIAM HUGHES
Monday morning

The *Fair Penitent*, II, i. Lady Vesey played the role of the faithless Calista who spoke these precise words in the play.

LETTER XXVIII

From Montague Belville, Esq., to John Evelyn, Esq.
BELMONT CASTLE

EVELYN—I have done the deed!—The villain has paid with his forfeit life the ruin of my Georgiana.—Oh! my friend—that spotless innocence, that paradise of ever-blooming sweets has been disgraced—dishonoured—ravished—by Colonel Neville, that monster in human shape—that villain—that—but this arm has stretched him breathless on the plain; he lives not to mock our sufferings, or to triumph in his villainy.

Last night, I flew at the appointed hour to the shrubbery where I found, as I thought, my Georgiana, eagerly expecting my arrival with all the impatience of the tenderest love.—I caught her in my arms and *hurried* her into the chaise, which drove off like lightning—for two hours she observed the most profound silence which I, ideot as I was, attributed to the agitation of her spirits. At last, a violent jolt of the chaise, caused by a rut in the road, terrified my companion, and she exclaimed in the wildest emotion "Oh, Heavens!" So unlike was this exclamation to the music of my charmer's well-known voice that two thousand frightful suspicions two thousand alarming ideas rushed at once upon my soul Luckily, I had in my pocket one of Dr. J. Brown's patent machine for striking light in a moment[1]—I drew it forth with trepidation

---

1. The following advertisement in the *Morning Post* (March, 1778) gives us contemporary information on the reform of the old tinder box, flint and steel matches:
   'FOR TRAVELLERS, MARINERS, ETC.; PROMETHEAN FIRE AND PHOSPHORUS
   G. Watts faithfully acquaints the public, that he has prepared a large variety of machines of portable, durable kind, with Promethean fire, paper and match inclosed, most admirably calculated to prevent those disagreeable sensations, which frequently arise in the dreary hour midnight, from the sudden alarm of thieves, fire or sickness; as by procuring an instantaneous

nd lighting the waxen taper, discovered, to my inexpressible tor-
nent, features I had never beheld before.— "Who art thou?" cried
I—almost frantic with desperation, "and where is my
Georgiana?—Which of you have conspired against my peace?—
and what envious, blasting hand hath thus insulting dashed the
cup of blessing from my lips? Whither shall the wild, distracted
Belville turn him? Where shall he seek his poor, abused, deluded
Georgiana? Stop fellow," cried I to the postillion in voice of thunder, at the same time striking out the glasses and bursting open
the door of the chaise—"Stop this moment"—my companion, in
an agony of terror at my ravings, could scarcely articulate in faultering accents, "Colonel Neville has deceived you—and is now with
your Georgiana—on the road to—London."—Uttering the words
she fell into a swoon, from which the hurry of my despair would
not allow me to recover her.—Wild and raving like one distracted,
I mounted one of the chaise horses, harnessed as he was, and
bare-headed—with a loaded pistol in each hand, rode on at a furious pace—exclaiming aloud—now on the name of Neville, now
on that of my Georgiana.—And Oh, Evelyn! as if my tortured soul
stood in need of horrid objects to encrease its gloom—the storm
and rain beat about my bare, defenceless head; no friendly star
appeared—and the ill-omened bird of night[2] from the decayed
mouldering battlements of a ruined tower shrieked in the wild
and chilling tone of madness and despair!—In this distracted
manner did I ride on two hours, till my horse picked up a nail.[3]—
Judge *then*, my friend, of my situation.—I, at that moment, felt all
the torments of the damned—what could I do? Forced, alas! to
pursue on foot—my weak exertion could not keep pace with my
swifter revenge—at last—propitious heaven threw a farmer in my
way—I dragged him from his horse (all the time demanding of

---

light the worst calamities and depredations might often be prevented in families. Experience has
likewise proved this invention to be the first utility to travelling mariners and those who frequently
rise in the night-time, as they can with one of those matches procure light, instantly, without the
great expence and danger of burning a lamp or candle.'
Dr. James Brown was also an inventor of a patent medicine, Dr. Brown's powders.
Cf. 'And birds ill-omened', *The Fair Penitent*, II, i.
Characteristic deflation of the Gothic melodrama.

him my Georgiana, in accents that might have moved a stone t
pity). Instantly mounting his steed, I flung my purse at the poor
fellow's head, and set off in full gallop, still more impetuous than
before;—at length, passing over a wild deserted heath, my ears
were alarmed by the piteous shrieks of a female—every cry went to
my soul.—"Perhaps," cried I in phrenzy, "this female may be
Georgiana, my love, sinking under the brutal violence of a tyrant
ravisher—perhaps, this very moment, he inhumanly riots in her
heavenly charms, whilst the lovely distracted mourner calls in vain
for succour, and pierces the unpitying air with cries for Belville to
relieve her!"—Love, rage, indignation and despair gave wings to
my impetuosity—I drove onward to the house from whence the
shrieks proceeded—the guilty door yielded to my force—I rushed
up stairs, and in my hurry and confusion, Oh Evelyn!—cut my
shin against the balustrade!—Adieu for a few moments, I am sent
for by my beloved.

In continuation
As I reached the room, the tumult of my soul scarcely allowed me
to perceive the accursed Neville, who stood prepared to oppose
my passage; a look of horror, which he could not disguise, told me
in the most forcible language that the deed was committed;
rushed by him regardless of a loaded pistol which he held in hi
hand, and bursting through the door, good heavens, what were m
feelings?—Gods! hadst thou, my Evelyn, but seen the beauteous
injured girl, her hands locked in a close embrace—her bright eye
immoveably fixed, while from them descended copious floods o
briny tears.—Astonished, petrified at the sight, I stood for som
moments motionless; at last, "Oh, my Georgiana!" I cried, "dos
thou not know thy faithful Belville? Oh, speak my Georgiana
speak to thy distracted Belville."—The lovely mourner, for
moment, cast on me a wistful look—heaved a sigh that seemed t
issue from the bottom of her soul, and resumed her former pos
tion; at this moment, wrought up to a pitch of desperation, I seize
a pistol, which I had laid upon the table, and calling to the detes
ed Neville, "Wretch," said I, "prepare to receive that punishmer
due to thy unequalled crimes." The monster, with an appearanc

of indifference, nodded consent, and taking our ground, my first ball went through his head; the noise of the pistols brought up his servant, with the people of the house; they instantly ran to assist the unhappy wretch, who seemed to be in his last agonies;—with difficulty he got out these words:—"Oh, Belville, I have fallen justly—conjure the injured Georgiana to forgive—Oh, heaven! have mercy—have mercy!"—his voice failed him—and after the most excruciating agonies, which lasted about seven minutes, he expired.—Thus, Evelyn, have I, in some small degree, avenged the wrongs of that angel.—So excessive was her stupefaction that even this scene of blood was unnoticed: every effort that was possible I made use of to awaken her from this lethargy, but in vain. Finding it impossible to restore her, and unable to procure any assistance, I removed her to the carriage, and with all the caution possible, drove her back to the Castle. During all this time she remained perfectly senseless.—But when we at length arrived, Oh Evelyn! the scene that followed! Her venerable father, on the news of her arrival, rushed out, and clasping her in his arms, had scarcely uttered the name of child when, awakened by his paternal voice, she uttered a scream that pierced the very walls of the castle; and, for near an hour, did she continue such agonizing cries as filled every heart with amazement and with horror. Her brother on one side, holding her folded in his arms, and Cecilia on her knees, endeavouring to soothe her agitated soul, her noble father seated on the other side—such a groupe—Sir James Dashton running from one apartment to the other, summoning the domestics and dispatching them for assistance; while thy Belville, astonished by grief, was calling on the name of his beloved, and acting the part of the most frantic Bedlamite.—At length, a neighbouring physician arrived; he ordered the suffering angel immediately to be brought up to her chamber, and none but her sister and the necessary attendants to be admitted; here, by the assistance of medicine, he restored her to a state of calmness.

In this interval, the rest of the family being collected, Mortimer, with looks of the most frantic impatience, conjured me to collect my thoughts, and to unveil to them this dreadful mystery.—During the horrid recital, the various feelings of my auditors were strongly depicted on their countenances; but the horror of the Earl, and the wild, furious air of Mortimer, exceeded all description; when I came to that part of my narrative which related to the fall of Neville, Mortimer, clasping me in his arms, exclaimed, "O, my Belville! well hast thou revenged the wrongs of our house. But how, how shall we reward thee?"—"Give me my Georgiana," I exclaimed, "intercede with thy noble father, and let all that is past be forgotten."—"Generous young man!" cried the Earl, "and canst thou ask her, dishonoured as she is?—Thy noble sentiments bespeak thy illustrious descent, and if my Georgiana survive this fatal day, I promise she shall be thine. But much, much do I fear—" Here the agonizing thoughts of his beloved daughter cut short his speech.

Oh, my Evelyn, my head is distracted, I reel—my brain grows giddy, the calmness that hitherto supported me is gone.—Pray for us, my Evelyn!—pray for my Georgiana, pray for thy

BELVILLE

Tuesday, October 23, 1787
P.S. Might I trespass so far on the goodness of my Evelyn as to request him to send down a bottle of Goulard's vegeto-minera water,[4] and some gold-beater's leaf for my shin,[5] which, in spite of my woes, I feel at times intolerably painful. Alas, my friend, such is the condition of humanity.—

---

4. Cf. *Treatise on the Affects and Various Preparations of Lead for Chirurgical Disorders,* trans. from the French, 3rd. ed. with additions by G. Arnaud (London, 1772), in which various treatments of this kind for skin disorders and bruises are prescribed. A new edition of 1777 is listed in the Dix Catalogue, along with *Belmont Castle.*
5. Liquid gold used to paint wounds; lead lotion (*liquor plumbi*) was used to treat bruises. More recently, silver has been used.

LETTER XXIX

From Lord Clairville to Lady Myrtilla Middleton
BOULOGNE-SUR-MER

Feb. 21

MY dear Myrtilla,

The agony of my mind, the fatigue of my body, and the pain of my wound altogether oppress, and sink me so that I can scarcely muster strength to guide my pen; yet, as I know your tender nature will be anxious to hear a full account of my *rencontre* with the late unhappy Scudamore, I sit down to write to you, even in the teeth of a peremptory mandate to the contrary[1] from my surgeon.—On the unfortunate night of my dishonour, I went to the Pantheon, wrapped in a black domino, with a mind tortured with rage, suspence and jealousy.—It was not long ere I discovered the unhappy Scudamore, and that guily wanton, whom I cannot name with temper, in close conversation,[2] and watched them with the vigilance of an Argus.[3]—In the hurry and confusion of the place I however lost sight of them; in vain did I rush through every room in search of them, frantic and agonized—the perturbation of my mind rose to distraction—my whole frame shook with tortures to which those of damned spirits are bliss and transports—the cold sweat stood in beads on my forehead—my knees tottered under me, and in the anguish of my soul I cursed Scudamore, that abandoned woman, my own existence and the ill-starred hour that gave me birth. My strength failed me—the room seemed to turn

---

. Martin was accused of promoting a duel with Lord George Fitzgerald in spite of an impeachment.
. The charge Martin brought against Mr Petrie was one of 'criminal conversation'.
. Cf. 'This wretched Argus of a jealous husband', *The Fair Penitent*, III, i.

around—the light danced before my eyes—my ears rung and had I not run precipitately to the sideboard and swallowed a large glass of champaigne, I had inevitably fainted. A little recruited by this refreshment, I threw off my domino, flung myself into my carriage and drove off instantly for Soho—on my enquiring below and describing the persons, I was convinced they were in the house; and drawing my sword, ran up stairs calling aloud the name of Scudamore—at the first landing place I struck my foot against the door, which flying open, discovered, oh, misery unspeakable! Scudamore and my wife. He instantly seized his sword and stood on his defence.—I attacked him with all the fury of a desperate maniac; his temper was superior to mine, his skill at least equal, and the combat was long and obstinate. At length with one furious *allonge* he passed his sword through my body up to the hilt—I instantly seized the shell with my left hand, and, being thus master of his weapon, levelled mine directly at his heart: pushing with all the strength remaining to me—I ran him through but missed my purpose—I drew it forth and pressed it again thro' a second place, and my wound and wrongs depriving me of all humanity and indeed reason, I again drew it back and ran him through a third time;—then, and not before, he sunk down at my feet exclaiming faintly—"Make your escape instantly, my Lord—I am but a dead man; alas! my poor Eliza!"—The fury that had hitherto transported me sunk at once when I saw my enemy stretched and swimming in his blood before my eyes, and I fell senseless into a chair behind me. How long I remained in the swoon, brought on by loss of blood and the unspeakable anguish of my mind, I know not; but on the recovery of my senses I found myself in bed in a strange room, which I since learn was at an inn on the road to Dover.—I was removed by slow journies hither. My wound is still intolerably painful, but I find my strength return, tho' slowly—my peace of mind is gone for ever!

CLAIRVILLE

LETTER XXX

From the Hon. C.F. Scudamore to Colonel Neville

The following letter to Colonel Neville, not arriving until after the death of that gentleman, was opened by his executors.

Two o'clock
MY dear Colonel,
ALL is over—the fortune of Clairville has prevailed and your friend will soon be numbered with the dead!—my life ebbs apace, my pulse sinks, my eyes grow dim, and the cold damp dew of dissolution hangs upon my forehead.[1]—My poor Eliza too!—alas, how are all my fond hopes of felicity blasted in the bud. When I wrote thee my heart beat high with expectation, and my guilty imagination glowed with fancied raptures; but mark the end—the vengeance of a wronged husband has stretched me in early youth on the bed of death, from which I fear I never more will rise. But my decaying strength will not allow me to be more particular.— William has orders to communicate the whole to you in person.

* * *

Four o'clock
As I find myself going, and my wounds very painful, with a view to hereafter, as an opiate to conscience, and an anodyne to my bodily ailments, I have sent William out for a good book called the *New Spiritual Magazine or Evangelical Treasury*, and he reads in broken accents, as distinctly as his tears will permit, most comfortable

---

1. Cf. *The Sorrows of Young Werther*, 2 vols (Dublin, 1787–8), II, p. 134.

passages about the New Jerusalem, heart-grace, heart-knowledge, faith, regeneration, justification, sanctification, glorification, and other strong cordials for fainting souls.—All which is very affecting and I edify prodigiously—but I find myself grow too weak to proceed further and I have ordered a couple of beef kidnies, and some porter—adieu, I see they are ready.

* * *

Six o'clock
I find myself sufficiently refreshed, tho' every moment filches away a little of my strength, to address a few words more to my Neville— I have arranged all my temporal affairs, and added a codicil to my will, bequeathing a sum for the endowment of an alms-house, for twelve blind men, and twelve gouty women.[2]—Oh my Eliza!— poor, dear, suffering angel—but we shall meet again!—the shock of seeing her Scudamore fall has been I fear too great for her gentle spirit.—Oh my love, my love, why must I leave you?—but it will not be—my life is gone, and I have hardly any strength to bid my friend a last adieu!—Oh, Neville, Neville, pity the agonies of thy departing Scudamore—alas! alas! I am afraid to die—my soul shrinks with horror from the thought of dissolution—yet what remedy?—I can no more—the cold hand of death is on me— Adieu—adieu—for ever![3]

C.F. SCUDAMORE

---

2. See Introduction, n.14, for an account of similar philanthropic gestures.
3. Cf. *The Sorrows of Young Werther*, II, p. 136.

LETTER XXXI

From Miss Juliana Blandford
to Lady Georgiana Shirley
GROSVENOR SQUARE

ALAS! my friend, how shall I describe the *comble* of grief, misery and distraction in which this wretched family is plunged!—how shall I bring the pen to write the shame which the late unhappy misconduct of Lady Clairville has brought on her dear, venerable parents—the good Sir John, with desperate hand, tears away from his hoary head the few grey tresses which the iron hand of the great destroyer, Time, had spared; Lady Fillamar sits like another Niobe[1] in senseless, stony stupor!—while the guilty yet still lovely authoress of all this woe raves in all the wildness of frantic desperation!

My Georgiana has doubtless heard how Lord Clairville surprised her with Mr. Scudamore, in a very improper house in Soho Square; a rencontre instantly ensued; his Lordship, though desperately wounded, was victorious, and the unhappy Scudamore fell.—Her Ladyship, who fainted instantly on the entrance of Lord Clairville, was carried home to her father's house, where she has ever since remained; but the agitation of her spirits, the consciousness of her blasted reputation, the censure of the severe, the pity of the good, and the last, I fear not least, the loss of her dear Scudamore, have deprived her sovereignty of reason,[2] and she now exhibits the most mournful spectacle in existence, the human mind, that master-piece of the deity! that glorious pre-eminence of our nature! that beautiful and wonderful machine, alas! my

---

1. Cf. *Hamlet*, I, ii, 146, with its reference to the inconstancy of women.
2. Richard Martin claimed that only madness could have caused Lady Vesey to act with such perfidy (*Humanity Dick*, p. 80).

friend! unhinged, deranged, destroyed!—My tears blind me so that I must lay down my pen.

* * *

Three o'clock

The poor distracted mourner has just left me, but good Heavens, how distressed, how dejected!—She has not, for an hour she spent in my room, spoken one connected sentence; yet still the superiority of her beauty appears, lovely even in its ruins.—She entered the chamber with a hurried step; her dress was of the whitest sattin, her thick auburn tresses hung neglected down and shaded her ivory forehead with a profusion of native ringlets; her face was pale; her eyes were sunk, yet beaming forth an unsteady vivacity which spoke but too plainly the state of her mind; her figure is, even already, emaciated, and her voice hollow and feeble.—"Hark!" exclaimed the beauteous phantom, in accents scarcely mortal. "Hark! Scudamore! my love! will you not shield me from the fury of my Lord?—indeed he will be angry with me—very angry— where is my love?—do not hide him from his poor Eliza, do not— sure he will come—oh, I had built him such a cottage, and made it so fine with lillies and roses, and trimmed the windows with eglantine and creeping jessamine, but my cruel Lord came and destroyed it all—was it not unkind?—Ah, who is this?"—then looking piteously on the floor—"see, see how it flows in torrents—oh save me, save me, save me"—and she fell into the arms of her woman. For a short time she remained insensible, but soon awaked again to life and misery; "No," she cried, "not yet, not yet!—pray, pray take care—tread softly, and do not awake him—my poor love is ill, and yet how charming he looks!—Ah, Scudamore, how could you leave me so unkindly?—you do not love, I fear, else sure you would not break the heart of your poor Eliza that doats on you— alas, my life, why do you look so pale?[3]—sure you are ill—I am not well myself—my heart is heavy! my poor heart too is strangely dis

---

3. Cf. 'Why dost thou look so pale?', *The Taming of the Shrew*, II, i, 143.

ordered"; and she put both her snowy hands to her forehead and remained a few moments silent; then starting from her reverie, "Bring me to my father," she cried, "I am innocent. Indeed I am— let him not believe my Lord, my cruel Lord!—he says I have wronged him—sure my father will not hate me too—he will not reject his child, nor cast her off to misery and ruin! oh, my heart, my poor heart!" and she sighed as if her bosom were bursting. A profuse shower of tears came to her relief which I hoped would to some degree calm the tempest in her soul;[4] but alas, her reason is gone, I fear, irrecoverably.—She still continued to look round her with the same wildness, and raved with the same incoherence.

* * *

Monday, 2 o'clock
ALAS! my friend, the event I feared has come to pass—the youthful, the beauteous, the elegant Lady Clairville is no more!—the working of her mind was too powerful for the delicate machine which contained it, and thus has she fallen an early sacrifice to the sensibility of her heart and the acuteness of her feelings. I will spare my friend a description, to which I feel myself unequal, of her parting moments—her wild insanity continued to the instant of her dissolution, and her last breath was spent in calling on the name of Scudamore.

Oh, may our sex by her fate be warned against the insidious arts of the vile deceiver—*man*, that destroyer of our happiness, who with specious guise and fair exterior lures us to our fall, then throws us like a worthless weed away.—

> "Base man the ruin of our sex was born,
> The beauteous are his prey, the rest his scorn;
> Alike unfortunate our fate is such,
> We please too little, or we please too much."[5]

---

4. Cf. 'blown up by tempest of the soul', *King John*, V, ii, 50; 'O then began the tempest to my soul', *Richard III*, I, iv, 44.
5. Unidentified.

LETTER XXXII

From Lady Myrtilla Middleton to Lord Clairville

OH, tyrant, monster!—give me back my Scudamore!—What!—I love thee? Dolt, ass, blockhead, ideot!—dost thou imagine any woman could be enamoured of such a wretched thing as thou art?—Give me my Scudamore—you have murdered him!—thy base heart would have trembled to have met him fairly in the field—restore him, monster, to these longing arms!—Why did my jealousy prompt me to betray to a cuckold—a horned monster—my life, my love, my Scudamore?—Thou wert too base a rival, even to alarm my beloved—confusion and plague light on thee—my memory fades—but still—that I could admit Clairville, that hated villain, to these arms, hangs on—wounds my recollection.—Hark!—did you not hear a noise? It is the voice of my Scudamore.—See! yonder, how he stalks—his hair of an end, bloody, disfigured, pale, pale, pale! See, he points to his wounds—shakes his goary locks[1] at the murdering Clairville, and glares with livid eye-balls on the guilty Myrtilla—my blood freezes—I faint—I faint—I faint—Oh, Oh, Oh, Oh!—

* * *

What shriek was that?—Was it an owl or a Canary-bird?[2]—Hark!—it was the ghost of Scudamore!—What, again!—Oh, don't shriek so, my love!—that bleak mountain is too cold for thee to rest on—don't shriek so—and I'll warm thee in my bosom—now, now I

---

1. Cf. 'never shake/Thy gory locks at me', *Macbeth*, III, iv, 51.
2. The bird, a member of the finch family, was brought from the Canary Islands in the eighteent' century. In Richard Martin's extended menagerie, 'dogs, cats and canaries were passed around—like so many picture postcards.' (*Humanity Dick*, p. 8.)

clasp thee—closer, closer still; avaunt, avaunt!—thou art the murthering Clairville; thy hand is red with the blood of my Scudamore;
wipe it in my heart? No, murderer; the black curtains of hell will
serve thee for a napkin; what shall be done to her who betrayed
her love?—Send hither my charmer—drag him hither by a cob-
web; his betrayer shall kiss his poor wounded bosom, and draw the
sword of murder from his heart.—What bloody fingers are
those?—Let me untwist them from the hair of my beloved—hark,
hark!—a shriek—a shriek again!—murdering monster—black,
cruel ruffian!—Smell this bouquet; do, pray my Lord, smell it.—It
is a nosegay of the sweet nightshade I have made for my
beloved.—Oh, my poor heart breaks;—murthering, inhuman
Clairville! Confusion seize on you, myself, and all the world.—
Yonder's a precipice; I see my charmer at the bottom. I come—I
come! 'Tis but a jump; and my beloved shall catch me in his arms.[3]

---

3. Tone acted in J. Home's play *Douglas* in Galway in 1783. The Martins had the leading roles.
Matilda, played by Lady Vesey, perhaps echoed here as Myrtilla, is reported, on the death of
Douglas, to have flown

> 'like lightning up the hill,
> Nor halted 'til the precipice she gained
> ... and headlong down' (Act V, i).

LETTER XXXIII

From Lord Mortimer to John Evelyn, Esq.
BELMONT CASTLE

THE cup of misery is full, and thou, yes, thou my Evelyn, must taste of the bitter draught. Thy friend Belville, and, oh my bursting heart—Georgiana, both, my Evelyn, both are numbered with the dead.—When I look back, my friend, to no very distant period, when I review those scenes of joy which my buoyant imagination had painted, and when I consider the sad reverse—when I behold a much loved sister torn from our fond embrace—a venerable father weighed down with sorrow to the grave—a noble youth, whose virtues would have been an ornament to any station, cut off by the iron hand of despair, and all, all in the space of a little month,[1] oh, Evelyn, dost thou not wonder at my philosophy?—'Tis that alone, 'tis the confidence in an All-wise Being, 'tis the duty which I acknowledge of supporting an aged father, and a solitary grief-worn sister, these considerations, these only can uphold me.

* * *

Nature must have her course; I was forced to give a few moments to grief. In the briefest manner possible will I unfold to you the fatal catastrophe, as I would spare you every needless affliction.— After the efforts of the physician had restored my darling Georgiana to a state of calmness, we entertained hopes, alas, ill-founded hopes, of her recovery; under this delusion we formed deceitful schemes of our future happiness. The ill-fated Belville

---

1. Cf. *Hamlet*, I, ii, 147.

entertained too noble sentiments of Georgiana to be affected by what was past; her mind, he knew, was the mind of an angel—all was fixed and the moment of her recovery was to unite them in indissoluble bonds. I undertook to inform our Georgiana of those intentions, and, having taken every proper precaution, I told her our design.—She was raised in her bed by pillows, clad in white pure as her mind, and twelve yards of muslin shaded her pale wan face. With angelic calmness did she hear me, and her reply, which was rather divine than human, is imprinted in indelible characters on my heart. "Your manly sense, my Edward, will let me speak the melancholy truth to you with greater freedom than I could to other members of the family. Don't amuse yourself with deceitful hopes. It is impossible I should recover. Already do I feel the cold hand of death upon me."—Oh, Evelyn, guess my sensations! the lightning from heaven could not have struck such horror in my soul. The angelic girl perceived my feelings; "Oh, my Edward, let me conjure you by everything sacred to support a manly fortitude—consider the duty that is now imposed on you; my father, my Cecilia, my Belville, all will look up to you for comfort. I know the ardency of your affection, you have always been the fondest of brothers—I know the pangs you will feel. But, my Edward, let that fortitude which you always possessed support you; exert yourself to quell that storm of affliction which I fear is ready to burst on you." The grief and horror that oppressed me did not allow me to interrupt her. "I have much to say to you, my Edward—I know the goodness of your heart, I know your kindness for the ill-fated Belville—continue it to him, my brother, tell him his Georgiana loved him to the last, and tell him as he regards my memory, I command him to avoid all extremity of grief. There is still something near my heart— oh, 'tis my Juliana; thou knowest not, my Edward, half the worth of that amiable girl; thy increasing fondness for her is one of my greatest consolations. Our fond father I know will consent to your union, and I desire this event may be no delay to its completion. I fear—I dread the feelings of that too sensible girl—assuage her grief, my Edward, and call in the aid of philosophy and religion to moderate her transports." Here the fatigue of her exertions overcame my angel—and she fell into a fainting fit.

She recovered by degrees, when the physician, calling me aside, told me that he thought it useless any longer to delay the awful truth—that her life was ebbing apace, and that a few hours would rob us of our Georgiana—he therefore advised me to communicate the fatal intelligence to the family. I hurried from the room and flew to the garden to give vent to my transports and prepare for the direful office. When I had gathered some resolution I returned to the parlour, where the whole family was collected—their countenances expressed the eagerest impatience, but soon did they gather from mine the fatal intelligence. Over this scene, Evelyn, I must draw a veil—the bare recollection of it harrows my soul—but think—picture to thyself my situation, endeavouring to smother my feelings, and to calm the rage of their affliction—with wonder, with astonishment do I look back on my fortitude, under a trial the bare idea of which makes my brain go giddy.

For two hours did an awful silence prevail, when a message from Georgiana summoned us to her apartment—but here too, my Evelyn, must I be silent; the pangs of that last, parting scene, are too dreadful to be related. With the most angelic composure did the dying Georgiana address us, and after bidding a last farewell to each of us in particular, conjuring us to restrain our grief and soliciting her father's blessing, she called me to her and desired me to endeavour to bring them away, as their lamentations would quite unfit her for the awful moment which she perceived was approaching.—But I must stop, my Evelyn, my sorrow must have vent.

* * *

In a few moments after my return my Georgiana died in my arms.—Oh, God! how hast thou visited us! Overcome by horror and the violence of my exertions to smother my feelings—I fainted away, and for forty minutes did I remain in that senseless condition; but the shrieks of woe soon assailed my ears. Vain were all my efforts, their transports were too violent to be restrained. The unhappy Belville alone displayed a calmness that gave me hopes, alas deceitful hopes.—Evelyn! thou hast lost thy friend; the enclosed letter which we found on his table will tell thee too much—and spare me the pang of relating the horrid particulars.

In a few days I shall write to you again—at present my heart is too full. Would to heaven that you were here to assuage the violence of our grief and give some consolation to

Thy afflicted,
MORTIMER

OH, Evelyn! the bell tolls for Georgiana and Belville; the hearses come nodding onwards—the sable ministers of death approach, and soon!—in a little hour, will the cold earth receive them.

LETTER XXXIV

From Montague Belville, Esq., to John Evelyn, Esq.

[Enclosed in the foregoing]

DEAD! Evelyn, to be nailed up in a coffin, of wood, of lead, or perhaps, *cold, cold stone;* shut up in a pit so dark, so damp, so deep, so *chilling cold*![1] I had a friend, a cherubim;[2] her voice as soft as the zephyr, her eye was as the dew of morning; she died of a broken heart; I followed her to the door of the vault; when the light of the tapers grew more and more dismal, when the sexton had gone off, when the shrieks of the mourners sounded fainter and fainter on mine ear, when, at last, it died away, I threw myself on the damp, *cold* earth; my heart was smitten, rent, grieved, broken, torn, pierced, distracted;[3] but I neither knew what I was, nor what, alas! I might be. Death! vault! grave! I understand not the words! what are they my Evelyn?

Oh! my Georgiana, do you recollect the steel pin you sent me by Laura, when at church you could neither speak to me nor hold out your hand for the crowd? Half the night was I on my knees before that pin; it was the dear pledge of affection. The world itself, the great globe shall pass away,[4] and time shall be extinguished; but eternity cannot efface the *impression* which that pin made upon my soul. But why do I address my beloved? She is dead, cold, cold; no more shall these arms encircle her waist, or these lips

---

1. Cf. *Werther*, ch. xx: 'Dead Charlotte, shut up in a pit, so deep, so cold, so dark'; and *The Fair Penitent*, V, i:'Cold! dead and cold!'
2. Cf. *The Fair Penitent*, II, i: 'Hads't thou been honest, thou'st be a cherubim.'
3. Cf. *Werther*, ch. xviii: 'My heart was smitten, grieved, rent.'
4. *The Tempest*, IV, i, 153: 'The solemn temples, the great Globe itself, / Yea, all which it inher it, shall pass away.'

tremble upon hers. Forgive, forgive! Oh, Evelyn, forgive me, for-give me! Yet, she still is mine; Georgiana is mine for ever; no, my Georgiana, we shall not be annihilated; yes, my Georgiana, from this moment you are mine. I fly to meet you; we shall see one another again; we shall see Neville in torments. We shall see your mother—I shall see her—I'll engage I shall find her out, and I shall not be afraid to shew her my heart; your mother, your image!

I have sent, Evelyn, to borrow the blunderbuss which hangs over the chimney-piece in the great-hall, for a journey; I go to dis-charge my debts, and pack up my trunk.—What, if the d——d shoemaker should not bring his bill! Adieu.

* * *

Past eleven o'clock
I have ordered my fire to be made up, and a pint of wine to be brought me. I thank thee, Heaven! that thou grantest me warmth in my last moments.

I draw near to the window, my friend, and through clouds which are driven rapidly along, I spy some stars; heavenly bodies! you shan't fall.—I have also seen the greater bear, favourite of all the constellations,[5] since it recalls your image to my view.

I beg you will protect my remains—at the far corner of the church-yard there are two willows; it is there I wish to rest; but, per-haps, good Christians will not chuse that their bodies should be interred near the corpse of an unhappy miserable wretch like me.—Ah, let me then be buried in Elwood Farm, in some sequestered valley or by the side of a purling stream, where the enamoured youth and love-lorn maiden may pour out their souls in plaintive tenderness, and bedew, with the soft tears of sympathy, the green sorrel that covers my grave.—Evelyn, I do not now shud-der that I hold in my hand the blunderbuss, the fatal instrument of death.

---

5. Cf. *Werther*, II, p. 117. Werther to Charlotte: 'I have also seen the greater bear—favourite of all the constellations.'

Half past eleven

I have put in the powder, yet still do I draw back—I wish to be buried in the clothes I now wear—Georgiana has touched them, and they are sacred.—I have on me an orange coat, with a blue cape and mother-of-pearl buttons—a waistcoat of pea-green sattin—and breeches of purple velvet—my pockets are not to be searched—the steel pin must be buried with me—I have stuck it in my waistcoat next my heart.

* * *

Three quarters past eleven

I have put in two slugs—will they hurt me, my Evelyn?—The clock srikes twelve—the blunderbuss is cocked—I go, Georgiana! Georgiana!—Evelyn, Evelyn!—Farewell, farewell, farewell, farewell!—for ever—Oh! Oh!—

LETTER XXXV

From Lord Mortimer to John Evelyn, Esq.
BELMONT CASTLE

THIS is, indeed, the house of mourning.—Oh, Evelyn, thy creative fancy would in vain attempt to picture such a scene of woe;
the *storm* of affliction, indeed, is past, but a still and gloomy horror, a *tranquility* more dreadful than the most outrageous whirl-
wind of passion, hath succeeded. That festive board, where mirth
and gladness once presided, how changed! how saddened!

To add, if it were possible to add, to our sorrows—Sir John and
Lady Fillamar, with their lovely Juliana, arrived here on Tuesday—
you know the afflictions of this amiable family—and you know, my
friend, the enthusiasm of affection which united the hearts of my
lamented sister and Juliana.—There is a luxury in grief, and in its
most exquisite state do we enjoy it.—The delicate sensibility of my
Juliana, for such do I hope to call her, is most feelingly alive to the
woes of a brother lamenting the sister of his affection. Doubly, tre-
bly, is my heart united by this mournful event.—My noble father,
softened by affliction, relaxing from the pride of family distinction, perceives and feels the excellence of that angelic maid.—Sir
John, left childless and forlorn, has adopted her as his daughter,
and settled on her his whole fortune. With a winning frankness
does she confess her love: "Yes, my Mortimer," did she say, whilst a
crimson blush overspread the lillies of her face—"I will tell you I
love my Mortimer, and most solemnly do I promise that no human
power shall alter my affection."—It was late in the evening, the
moon shone bright, the leafy trees spread an awful, gloomy shade,
and not a breeze disturbed the solemn stillness; she reclined on
my arm as we walked through the avenue of elms.—"Hear me,
bright moon!" I cried, as I threw myself on my right knee—"whilst

[137]

by thee, and yon twinkling stars, I swear to love, to adore the goodness of my Juliana:—angelic excellence!—How shall I repay thee?—How shall I deserve such worth?—And wilt thou, then, my Juliana!—wilt thou, one day, be mine?—Day of rapture! day of extatic bliss!—Crown my happiness, angelic as thou art—name the propitious day and complete the bliss of thy Mortimer."— "No, my Lord," she cried, "reflect but for a moment, and you will see the impropriety of your request.—Can Juliana …"

The gushing tears here stopped her utterance.—I felt her meaning.—"Angelic girl," I cried, "thy sensibility unmans me—I yield to thy just advice.—The memory of our Georgiana shall be respected."

Oh, Evelyn! felicitate me on my prospects—she will be mine.—Six sad months, though, are to be devoted to the memory of the lamented Georgiana; and then, then, my Evelyn, shall I be raised to the pinnacle of human happiness.

Sir James, by his unaffected sympathy in our afflictions, has completely won the heart of the lively Cecilia—his native good sense, too, is beginning to conquer that excessive foppery which once made him so ridiculous, though there is full enough of it to excite our mirth:—during the time of mourning he has displayed a singularity which to an indifferent spectator would appear rather laughable, tho' in our situation its absurdity passed unnoticed— he has become all at once extremely religious.—He attends Chapel regularly, every morning and evening, and he has composed two or three sermons which he read to us in the great hall.—So pleased was he with his performances that he entertained serious thoughts of going into the Church, where his talents for preaching, he thinks, would soon raise him to the highest station—and I verily believe that he would have posted off to the bishop of ——, who, you know, lives in our neighbourhood, to request he would ordain him, if I had not with great difficulty dissuaded him.—My father has consented to his union with Cecilia and it is to take place at the same time with ours;—she is to have a fortune of £60,000.—My establishment is already fixed; my father, who is determined to live a very retired life, gives me the Portland Place house, together with Sherwood Hall and £12,000 a year. Sir John Fillamar, notwithstanding my most earnest remonstrances, insists on giving Juliana £20,000 and settling his whole estate upon her after his decease.

These prospects serve in some measure to dissipate our grief, but long must it be, my Evelyn, before it can pass away.—The form of my much-loved Georgiana, her charms, her virtues, her sufferings, the unhappy end of Belville; all, Evelyn, are still present to our view—their graves are still watered by our tears—the wounds inflicted by their untimely end still bleed, and from time alone, that grand healer of human ills, are we to hope for relief.—My father, Sir John and Lady Fillamar—Sir James—Cecilia—my Juliana—all solicit your company—is any other incentive necessary?—if there is—your presence is most ardently wished for by

Your faithful
MORTIMER

FINIS

BIBLIOGRAPHY

1. TEXT

Belmont Castle: or, Suffering Sensibility (Dublin, 1790), National Library of Ireland. One of the two extant copies known.

2. WORKS BY TONE

An Address to the People of Ireland (Dublin, 1796).
An Argument on behalf of the Catholics of Ireland (Dublin, 1791).
A Review of the Conduct of Administration (Dublin, 1790).
Life of Theobald Wolfe Tone, ed. W.T.W. Tone, 2 vols (Washington, 1826).
The Autobiography of Theobald Wolfe Tone, ed. R. Barry O'Brien, 2 vols (Dublin, Cork, Belfast, n.d.).

3. COMMENTARY ON *BELMONT CASTLE*

Dix, E.R. McClintock, *Catalogue of the Library of E.R. McClintock Dix*, National Library of Ireland, mss 5366.
Mc Manus, M.J., 'When Wolfe Tone Wrote a Novel', *Irish Press* (24 December 1934), p. 10.
'The Man Who Stole Wolfe Tone's Books', *Irish Press* (1 July 1942), p. 8.
A Bibliography of Wolfe Tone (Dublin, 1940).
O'Kelly, F., 'Wolfe Tone's Novel', *Irish Book Lover*, vol. 2 (March–April, 1935), pp. 47–51.

4. CONTEMPORARY MAGAZINES AND JOURNALS

Gentleman's and Citizen's Almanack, Registry and Directory (Dublin, 1784–9).
Hibernian Magazine (Dublin, 1788–1913).
The London Review (London, 1787–90).
Town and Country Magazine (Dublin, 1788–90).
Universal Magazine and Review or Repository of Literature (Dublin, 1790).

5. SECONDARY SOURCES

Anon., *A Short Review of The Recent Affair of Honour between His Royal Highness the Duke of York and Lieutenant Colonel Lennox by a Captain of the Company of One of the Guards* (London, 1789).
Anon., *The Fair Hibernian*, 2 vols (Dublin, 1789).

BIBLIOGRAPHY

Anon, *The British Music Miscellany*, 2 vols (London, 1734).

Ashton, J., *Old Times: A Picture of Social Life at the End of the Eighteenth Century* (London, 1885).

Ball, John, *Odes, Elegies, Ballads Etc.* (Dublin, 1772).

Ball, William, *Index to the Statutes at Large, Passed in the Parliament Held in Ireland*, 9 vols (Dublin, 1799).

——, (trans.) *Vert-Vert* by J.B. Gresset (Dublin, 1789).

Barrington, Jonah, *Personal Sketches of his own Times*, 2 vols (London, 1827–32).

Bence–Jones, M., *Burke's Guide to Country Houses* (London, 1978).

Blacker, Rev. B.H., *Brief Sketches of the Parishes of Booterstown and Donnybrook in the County of Dublin* (Dublin, 1834).

Burke, Sir J.B., *Dictionary of The Landed Gentry of Great Britain and Ireland*, 2 vols (London, 1954).

Burtchaell, G.B., & T.W. Sadleir, *Alumni Dublinenses* (Dublin, 1935).

Butler, M., *Romantics, Rebels and Reactionaries: English Literature and its Background 1760–1830* (Oxford, 1981).

Craig, M., *The Volunteer Earl* (London, 1948).

Crowest, F.J. (ed.), *The Story of the Flute* (London & New York, 1914).

Cullen, L.M., *The Emergence of Modern Ireland 1600–1900* (London, 1981).

Curran, William H., *Sketches of The Irish Bar*, 2 vols (London, 1855).

Dunne, J.P. (ed.), *Ninety-eight Club Notes: Miniature Memoirs of Wolfe Tone and Napper Tandy 1798–1898* (Dublin, 1898).

Dunne, T.W., *Theobald Wolfe Tone, Colonial Outsider* (Cork, 1982).

Edkins, J. (ed.), *A Collection of Poems*, 2 vols (Dublin, 1789).

Forster C., *Life of Bishop Jebb DD, FRS, with a selection of his Letters*, 2 vols (London, 1836).

Gerard, A., *Some Fair Hibernians* (London, 1897).

Goethe, J.W., *The Sorrows of Young Werther*, 2 vols (Dublin, 1780–81).

Goodwin, A., (ed.) *The New Cambridge Modern History*, vii (Cambridge, 1965).

Goold, T., *An Address to the People of Ireland on the Subject of the Projected Union* (Dublin, 1799).

——, *A Vindication of The Right Hon. Edmund Burke's Reflections* (Dublin, 1791).

Goulard, T., *Treatise on the Effects and Various Preparations of Lead for Chirurgical Disorders*, trans. G. Arnaud, (London, 1772; new ed. 1777).

Granville, M., *The Autobiography and Correspondence of Mary Granville, Mrs. Delany*, ed. Lady Llanover, 6 vols (London 1861).

Graves, R., *Recollections of William Shenstone* (London, 1788).

Hardy, F., *The Memoirs of Lord Charlemont* (London, 1810).

Home, J., *Douglas: A Tragedy* (Dublin, 1757, Belfast, 1766).

Inglis, B., *The Freedom of the Press in Ireland 1784–1841* (London, 1954).

Jebb, R., *A Letter of Remonstrance to Denys Scully Esq.* (Dublin, 1803).

——, *Arguments For and Against the Union* (Dublin, 1799).

Lee, N., *The Rival Queens* (London, 1677).

Leslie, Rev. J.B., *Clogher Clergy and Parishes* (Enniskillen, 1929).

Lodge, E., *Portraits of Illustrious Personages of Great Britain, with Biographical and Historical Memoirs of their Lives and Actions*, 20 vols (London, 1835).

Lodge, J., *The Peerage of Ireland, or a Genealogical History of The Present Nobility of That Kingdom* 7 vols, (London, 1789).

Lynam, S., *Humanity Dick: A Biography of Richard Martin M.P. 1754–1834* (London, 1975).

MacDonagh, O., *States of Mind: A Study of Anglo-Irish Conflict 1780–1980* (London, 1983 1985).

McDowell, R.B., *Irish Public Opinion 1750–1800* (London, 1944).

BIBLIOGRAPHY

Mc Kinnon, J., *The Services of the Coldstream Guards* (London, 1921).

Maxwell, C., *Ireland Under the Georges 1714–1830* (London, 1940).

National Gallery of Ireland, *Bicentenary of the College Historical Society 1770–1970* (Dublin, 1970).

O'Brien, D., *The History of the Earls of Inchiquin* (London, 1949).

O'Raifeartaigh, T. (ed.) *The Royal Irish Academy: A Bicentennial History 1785–1985* (Dublin, 1985).

Radcliffe, S., *A Serious and Humble Inquiry* (Dublin, 1727).

Rocque, J., *Survey of City, Harbour, Bay and Environs*, with improvements and additions by Mr. Bernard Scale (Dublin, 1777).

Rowe, N., *The Fair Penitent: A Tragedy* (Dublin, 1746).

Sampson, W., *A Faithful Report of the Trial of Hurdy Gurdy at the Bar of the Court of King's Bench* (Belfast, 1794).

Shenstone, W., *The Works in Prose and Verse* (Dublin, 1777).

——, *The Poetical Works of William Shenstone*, ed. G. Gilfillan (Edinburgh, 1854).

Smith, C., *Emmeline; or, The Orphan of the Castle*, 2 vols (Dublin, 1789).

Stanhope, P., *Letters of The Earl of Chesterfield to his Son* (London, 1774).

Synge, E., *A Letter to the Rev. Stephen Radcliffe, Vicar of Naas* (Dublin, 1725).

Taylor, W.B.S., *History of the University of Dublin* (London, 1845).

Union Tracts (Dublin, 1799) (Includes pamphlets by Jebb, Goold, Ball and others).

Vicars, A., *Index to the Prerogative Wills of Ireland* (Dublin, 1897).

Walsh, T.J., *Opera in Dublin 1705–1797: The Social Scene* (Dublin, 1973).Wapole, H., *The Correspondence of Horace Walpole*, ed. W.S. Lewis *et al.*, 42 vols (New Haven, 1937–81).

Wraxhall, Sir N., *Memoirs* (London 1818).

Wright, Sir W.B., *Ball Family Record: Genealogical Record of the Ball Family* (York, 1908).

ſ